Chapter 1- Talinda and Sonjay

Today was a typical day. I was home, wrapping up my webinar. I needed to put a rush on things so I could make it to my hot yoga class. I heard the alarm chiming letting me know my husband made it in for lunch. My profession was simple. I was a life coach. My husband, on the other hand, was trying to lay his tracks down in politics. Growing up, I never imagined being married to the mayor of Atlanta, let alone the new Governor of California.

We had been living in California for the past six years. I could hear him downstairs punching in the alarm code. Yes. I am one of those cliché wives that works from home and makes their schedule. My husband makes sure he comes home for lunch at least three times out the week to keep things spicy. I had to admit I was very proud of him. We had been together since middle school. I have watched a boy grow into one handsome man. I could hear his steady steps as he approached my office.

He tapped on the door lightly. We had a code. When the door was closed, do not disturb, and if the door looks cracked, just announce yourself, so I won't get scared. It was corky, but it worked. As he pushed open the door, I stood from my chair and wore the biggest smile on my face." Welcome home, baby!" I said, holding my arms out, wanting his embrace. "Hello, beautiful," he said, placing his juicy lips on mine. I had done well for myself. I loved my black man, and he was sexy as hell. As a kid, he was skinny and tall with freckles. He even had braces for our entire four years in high school. He stood before me now, six foot three inches tall. His freckles were still there, complementing his hypnotizing smile. His body had filled out over the years.

We stood there kissing passionately. Once he stopped embracing me, he spun me around, telling me sweet nothings about how beautiful I was. He knew how to make me feel special. We looked at each other in the mirror. There I stood five foot two compared to him I was a little person. I loved it, though. He would sweep me off my feet each time we hugged. I took our conversation and headed downstairs. I had his lunch already prepared, and it only needed its final touches. "So future Mayor of California, how was the promotional meeting this morning?" I asked.

I loved seeing him light up when he talks about his campaigning. I had to admit it was amazing seeing my man's name in the big lights. Mr. Sonjay Boyd is the future of California. Together we would do our part to make California great again. Hell, I had to laugh to myself on that one. Someone had to jump in and get their hands dirty to fight for our people. Our current president was about as dependable as a pair of flip flops on baby dee in the summertime. I continued to put the last few touches on the lamb gyro and Greek salad I had prepared for lunch. Jay was still telling me about the polls and how he wanted to get a good grip on the Caucasian community to vote for him. To do that, he needed me to help him.

It wasn't easy to get the majority vote from Caucasians. Jay had a lot of odds already against him. Being an African American male was already the first red flag, but I was never blessed to birth a child. Californians like to see a family in roles such as these. It's almost like selling them the perfect family dream. In our case, Jay was able to bring the cool Afrocentric super woke wife who could speak everyone's language no matter who you are. I had dozed off. When I snapped out of it, Jay was confirming if I heard the details for dinner tonight. "Of course, I will be there.

What kind of fundraiser would it be if Talinda Taylor-Boyd wasn't in the building? I wouldn't miss it for the world. I will fill the room with a few motivational quotes that will encourage them to reach deep into those pockets." I smiled while pecking him on the lips. I was going to support my man. We needed that money if he was going to win this campaign.

We wrapped up our lunch by making love. I was not going to make it to my hot yoga class. Things had gotten steamy enough, and I was able to check working out off my to-do list today. I was feeling productive as I watched Jay take a shower. I laid there, reflecting. Although we did not have children, I was full. Our souls connected, and surprisingly, after all this time, I have never stepped out on him. He has been my one and my only until death does us part. My thoughts were interrupted when I heard something vibrating. I looked around, moving the white comforter, trying to see where it was coming from. We usually don't bring phones in our bedroom. It has been a rule of ours for the last eight years.

The room was silent again, and the only sound I could hear was Jay humming a Boyz to Men song while he was in the shower. Before you knew it, I could hear the vibrating again. This time it caused me to hop up out of bed and start looking. His blue suit was neatly folded on the other side of the room on the white and gold accent chair. He usually keeps his things in that corner. The buzzing continued, whomever it was wanted his attention immediately. I quickly ruffed through his pants pocket until I finally felt a small cellular device. It surely wasn't the one we have just alike. I am sure it's a good explanation for why he has a new phone. I know politics can be a bit much. Who would want them to have access to your personal information?

The water had finally stopped, and I could hear Jay stepping out of the shower. His humming turned into the water from the sink running. It gave me enough time to quickly get his items back in order and hop in the bed unbothered. I did just that. He was coming out of the bathroom as I was just fluffing my hair. I had a few questions, but he had never given me any indication that I needed to worry about him stepping out on me. This new occurrence does, however, make me want to hit up my sister and get her thoughts on this.

"Penny for your thoughts?" Jay asked as he tied his towel around his waist. He walked over and kissed me on my forehead. "I still got you hot and bothered, I see." He asked. I had no idea what would give him that perception. I was no way in any kind of mood for round two. I smiled but didn't respond. He immediately noticed I had something on my mind that humor couldn't shake off. It didn't happen often, but once I had my mind on something, it would take a lot of convincing to get me to change it. I snapped back to reality and went to the hop in the shower. I desperately wanted to avoid this conversation until I talked to my sister. I know I have a good thing going, so I don't want to mess things up by bringing unnecessary drama to our household.

"Well, I guess we can discuss this later. I have to get back." I could hear Jay shouting from the bedroom, telling me his goodbyes. I responded, letting him know I would be home late. I had some things I needed to take care of. He didn't respond. Moments later, the alarm chimed, letting me know it was armed. I asked my Bluetooth speaker to play some India Arie because I needed to just vibe out on a positive note. I wanted to leave all negative energy in this shower.

I sang along for a few songs and finally decided I had been in concert long enough. I grabbed my white plush housecoat and slipped into my shower shoes. I was big on cleanliness. Everything had its place. Fresh feet on a bathroom floor was not a place my feet should be. I kept my tunes jumping as I bopped around the house. I opened the entertainment system and found my tablet. I wanted to hit up my sister to see what we could get into for the rest of the day.

She knew I was going to call her, that was always the first thing she said when she accepted the call. We were fraternal twins, and I was the oldest by two minutes. As twins, that point never went unnoticed. You would think we were identical, except our skin complexion was different. My hair is thick and curly, while hers was long and bone straight. I could always flat iron my hair, and I am sure I could give her a run for her money, but I tend not to entertain my sister too much. She had some issues in the past that brought a wedge between us.

"Rolindaaaaaaa? I said into the tablet showing all my pearly whites. "Hey, Talindaaaaaa!" She said in return. I unhooked the tablet and began to walk around the house, checking all the windows and doors. I always had an unsettling feeling when Jay left me. I continued my conversation with Roe when she finally said something that piqued my interest. She mentioned Tyesha's name, which was my best friend since I could walk. "Wait, Roe. Say that last part again." I asked, knowing that was a dead giveaway that I wasn't listening in the first place. I could tell by the look on her face she knew I wasn't. "Ok, you got me. I heard the majority of what you were saying. Just repeat the last part", I stated in a tone that indicated I was pleading my case. Knowing yet again, I couldn't pull the wool over her head.

We both shared a laugh as we knew she caught me, and it was no way around it. She started over from the beginning just to be petty. According to Roe, Tyesha had been going through a tough situation with her husband, Kyle. We all grew up together, and Kyle just so happened to be Jay's best friend. He was the best man at our wedding. He went out with the boys, including Jay. They bar hopped and then ended up at a

Gentlemen's club. I never care when they hit the town, but this night a girl was assaulted. It came back that Kyle was involved. Tyesha is a lawyer; the case came right to her desk. I can only imagine what my girl was going through.

I told Roe we needed to set up some time to kick it. I had quickly changed my mind about meeting her today. I needed to catch up with my homegirl and make sure she was ok. We said our goodbyes, and I placed the tablet on the kitchen counter. It dawned on me as Roe gave me the scoop, she kept mentioning Jay and Kyle versus just Kyle. I needed to talk to Ty because she was given the case. She knows the facts. Something like this could hurt Jay's campaign. Furthermore, I can't imagine him being caught up in anything like this.

It was time to get out of my plush robe and toss some clothes on. Once I made it up the stairs and into my room, I placed the tablet back in its rightful place. I saw something that caught my eye. It was something underneath the chair that Jay's suit was on. I looked around, and I quickly dropped to my knees to get what looked like a book of matches. I grabbed the item and sat on my knees as I examined the item. It was covered in cheetah print with a lady's stiletto on the front. It was a matchbook. It was clear he very well could have been with Kyle. The other side of the matchbook read El Fetche.

I had no idea where this place was. I honestly had never heard of it before. It was further confirmation that something was a little off this morning. I quickly grabbed a dress I could throw on, and I slipped into my Nike slides. I was not in the mood to be super cute, but somehow once I put on some wooden accessories and picked my hair out. I had to admit. I was bad. I sincerely hope Jay is not involved in this mess. I am a firm believer in monogamy. I wouldn't have said "I DO" if it wasn't something I wanted to do. One thing he was not going to do was have me on the side as the trophy wife. I am not here to take pictures and do God knows what away from the cameras. We not white. We don't do that. I hate to toss that stereotype out there, but we all know there is a lot of things African American women will not put up with that they will.

Within minutes I was in my Land Rover and connected the Bluetooth. I sent a voice clip to Tyesha telling her I was coming over. It was still early in the day, so I knew she would be home. It was only going to take me a few minutes to get to her house. I thank goodness we made it out the projects as kids. Our parents struggled, and we made a promise to ourselves that no matter what, we were both going to be successful lawyers. She was able to make her wishes come true. I, on the other hand, put my life on a bit of a hold. The more I think about it. I can't blame that on Jay. I decided to give up. It was the best thing to do. He was also in school, but the loans had gotten too much for me to pay for. Jay wasn't working at the time, so I put my stuff on the back burner.

Just thinking of the repulsive things Jay could have been doing makes me regret letting myself go. My mother would be turning in her grave right now. Ty's mother was our God-mother, and our moms were the best of friends. You would have thought they were blood sisters. We grew up in Decatur. Things weren't handed to us. Our moms were repeat criminals that would team together to drug and rob men. One night they ran up on the wrong guy. They presented him with a threesome and spiked his drink. What they didn't know is he didn't drink. They snorted a few lines and played around a bit and did their routine. This man knocked out as scheduled, but during the process of snatching his jewelry, he woke up and shot them both.

This situation required no questions. It was all over the news. No one cared they left behind children with family members not stable enough to provide for them. We were lost.

If it weren't for our neighborhood that had so much respect for our mothers, we wouldn't have made it. We had to bust our asses to survive. Some of us made it through, and some didn't. Don't get me wrong; my father was around, but there is nothing like the security a mother provides. As my mind thought of many tragedies we had gone through, I was pulling up to Ty's house. She had done well for herself. I was proud of her, and her house was so lovely. It was a three-story home with an in-law suite in the back yard along with a pool.

Of course, we both lived in a predominately Caucasian neighborhood. However, Tyesha wanted to let it be known she had to stay. She purchased four acres and built her home throughout a year. She also went to the city and changed the street name. She renamed the street after her son Royalty. I laughed to myself as I unbuckled my seatbelt and gathered my purse. I kept my keys out and let myself in. I knew she was home. I saw her matching Rover in the driveway. I didn't see Kyles black Rover. They usually keep things nice and cute, but everything that looks good isn't right. We, as adults, must make lemonade out of those rotten lemons we sometimes get served.

"Ty! I shouted as I walked through the door. There was no way she was going to hear me from the ground floor. I removed my shoes before walking up the spiral staircase. She had a thing for white as well. I swear it feels like we were the twins. By the time I made it to the second floor, I was breathing super heavy. It didn't matter if I worked out every day or not. Those stairs would put a hurting on anyone. I called Ty's name once more. Again, there was no response. She was trying to kill me. I had to take a quick way out. I turned and pressed the purple elevator button. We had a thing for purple and grey.

I patiently waited for the elevator to reach me. Once the doors opened, I noticed I could hear someone upstairs. I pressed the penthouse button, and within a few seconds, the door was opening again. I stepped out into the atrium and called her name once more, and still, nothing. I walked around her golden Buda and went to search for my friend. She was starting to scare me by not responding. "Ty! I know you hear me!" I shouted, but this time I added a little more intensity behind her name. I finally reached her walk-in closet that leads to her master bathroom.

I saw her sitting in the corner of her closet by her shoe rack. She was in a black satin gown surrounded by shredded clothing, and it wasn't her stuff. She was sobbing intensely. I put down my bag on her island dresser. I needed her to know she was safe. She had extreme anxiety and could solve everyone's problems but her own. I continued to walk slowly towards her. She knew I was about to get on the floor and remove the scissors from her hands. Mascara was running down her eyes. She was hurt. I hadn't seen her like this since the time Kyle cheated in college and made the chick get an abortion.

"Ty, listen to me." We can talk about anything. What's going on, baby?" I asked as I was leaning in slowly, now taking my hand to remove the scissors. I successfully disarmed her. She was clearly in a disturbed state of mind. "Why, Tati? Why does he act like he is one of these busters in the hood?" Ty was now wiping her nose with some of Kyles's shredded ties. I didn't have the answers she was looking for. My concern was to get her up and out of the closet. "Come on, baby, let's go get something to eat," I said, trying to think of what would get her out of here. She never turned down a meal. I know she doesn't want to be in public right now, so I will go downstairs and see what I could whip up for us.

Surprisingly she agreed to come with me. I stood up and held my hand out to help her get up. She latched on, and we both counted to three, and I pulled her up. Once she was standing on her feet, I gave her a bear hug. I needed her to feel my energy and know that everything will be ok. We will get through this together, the same way we did back in the day. We stood there, embracing one another for what seemed like an hour. It didn't matter how long it was. I wasn't going anywhere until I knew she was ok. Once her tears slowed down and the sobbing became an actual voice, we held hands as we left the closet. Before we walked into her bathroom, and I lifted her head and told her to close her eyes. I walked her over to the vanity and sat her down, still instructing her to keep her eyes closed.

I dashed over to the linen closet and grabbed a washcloth and went to dampen it. I could hear her starting to sob once more, so I put a little pep in my step. I wrung out the washcloth and went to clean off her face. I put the warm compress on her eyes first and gently cleaned her face. "We can get through this; this isn't over. But once we face this storm, the other side will be so much greater." I did what I could to soothe her. "You don't know that." She said, shaking her head. She was hurt to her core. I ignored her comments. I knew there was nothing I could say that would sway her into changing her mind about things right now. So I moved on from the pain of it all and went straight into the facts.

"What happened, Ty?" I asked, now allowing her to open her eyes and join me by the sink. She slowly opened her eyes. Her reaction was a lot better than I expected. We had a rule, never to allow ourselves to see a broken reflection. Her eyes were puffy, but her make up was no longer a catastrophe. She turned and kissed me on my cheek. I returned the favor with a hug. She released me, and we both stared in the mirror. We were still holding hands. I turned to her and once more. "Answer my question," I said. She knew I was over the pity party and ready to get down to the nitty-gritty. Without saying a word, she led me out to her bedroom.

The white drapes were blowing in the wind as the curtains played peek a boo with the window. I chose to release her hand and sit down on the leather couch on the balcony. We walked out of the French doors, and we sat down. Before she got started, I knew things would be juicy, so I begged her to come downstairs so I could find something to eat. Sincerely, who doesn't like to eat when someone about to serve them some tea? She reluctantly gave me what I wanted, and we started chatting on the way down in the elevator. A month ago, the fellas decided to hang out. When she said fellas, I knew it was more than just Jay and Kyle involved. Back in the day when we all attended college together, we all hung tight. It was our thing to have a clique that was filled with couples.

It was a total of 6 couples when we first started. It slowly dwindled to three by the time we all graduated. The remaining few consisted of me, Ty, Jay, Kyle, Dionne, and Derrick. They were both males, and it was starting to happen more and more frequently. We accepted them with open arms. Years down the line, they both agreed to be straight and that what they experience was only a phase. Regardless they kept up their tight bond. Once we landed on the bottom floor. My mind was already about to bust wide open. They all were going out on the town to celebrate news about Dionne's unborn child. This was significant, considering Kyle was the only one with children.

They all ended up at the strip club, they were sloppy drunk and took some strippers to a hotel suite. The night got away from them all, and they started having sex. The next day the fellas wake up like everything is normal, ignoring the bloody sheets they were sleeping on. The ladies were able to leave the room once the fellas passed out. None of the other ladies have mentioned the incident except for one. She was beaten on top of having extremely rough sex. She felt violated and wanted to press charges against the man she slept with. Somehow, she ends up accusing Kyle. She has not provided the names of the other ladies.

By the time she was finished with the incident, I had already defrosted chicken breast to toss together a salad. I turned on the fire grill she had installed last year. It was convenient to be able to grill indoors without dying from smoke inhalation. Ty continued to tell me how the case landed on her desk. It had gone through a few public defenders that were not willing to take the case due to Tyesha's stellar reputation. She finally had the balls to approach Tyesha in her office the other day, demanding she takes her case. Once she sat down and laid her documents on the table, she had no other choice than to take the case in hopes of making it go away. Unfortunately, the young lady is not willing to go away.

I was cutting onions and couldn't tell if it was making me weep or if it was anger rising inside because Jay was involved. I wanted to know how did she know it was Kyle and not the other guys? I had so many things I wanted to ask but no longer wanted to press the issue. "So, what does Kyle have to say for himself?" I asked. I, at least, need to know that much. "He doesn't know. Client privilege I can't tell him. I am waiting right now for the Sherriff to ring my doorbell to arrest him. He is coming home in another hour or so. I just can't believe he would get caught up in something so scandalous?" She held her head low. It wasn't much I could do but pass the bottle of wine to her. It was no need to keep refilling the glass. It was time for the entire bottle.

I couldn't imagine being in her shoes. We sat in silence for a few minutes picking over our chicken salad. We both had suddenly lost our appetite. Our silence was interrupted by someone coming in the front door. We both stood up in shock. We could hear footsteps on the marble floor. Once they got loud enough, we were able to see it was Kyle. I dropped my fork at the sight of him, while Ty, on the other hand, was giving him a major side-eye. "Hey, beauties. Frick and Frack." Kyle greeted us with such a cheerful demeanor, not knowing that karma is a bad thing to toy with. "I think I am going to head out unless you need me to stay," I said, looking over to Ty for confirmation. She nodded her head, giving me the ok to leave. I dumped my plate and hers too. I knew she was not going to eat anything else now that Kyle was home. I rinsed the plates and bowls off and placed it in her dishwasher. I walked over and kissed her on the forehead.

I needed to run upstairs to grab my belongings. I was trying to move as quickly as I could before things got thick. I didn't even get to tell her about the phone that was vibrating earlier or the matchbook I found. I made it upstairs on the elevator, and once I landed and gathered my belongings, I made my way back down. I was all out of breath. My heart was beating super-fast. When the doors of the elevator opened, I could hear the two of them having a heated discussion. As I was putting on my shoes by the door, the doorbell rang. I froze. I was already in an awkward position. I had all the meat and potatoes of what was going down. They were just at the beginning of a long night. Kyle headed back towards me to open the door.

Frustration consumed his face. He snatched the door open, almost knocking me down if I hadn't stepped out of the way. Tyesha was also coming around the corner to see who had the nerve to interrupt their conversation. I tried to get past Kyle to get out of the door. I noticed it was the Sherriff. He was there to serve Kyle. I turned to Tyesha, who was standing there in disbelief. She had just said less than an hour ago she was dreading this moment. "Are you Kyle McNeil?" The sheriff asked.

"Yes, I am, but how can I help you?" Kyle said, looking confused. If silence could kill, we would all be dead. Everything from that point happened so quickly. "You have the right to remain silent. Anything you say can and will be used against you in the court of law." He began to Mirandize Kyle. "Wait! My lawyer is right there. You can't arrest me." Kyle shouted.

"Is this true?" Are one of you ladies this man's lawyer?" the sheriff asked. We both looked at each other. I shook my head, no. Tyesha, on the other hand, verbally made it clear she was not his lawyer; in this case, it would be a conflict of interest. Kyle turned and stared her down. "What do you mean, you're not my lawyer?" Kyle asked as he was shoved in the squad car. He didn't break his stare the entire time. As the squad car drove away, I wondered if Tyesha was going to bail him out. She quickly said no. It would be a conflict of interest. She asked if she could stay with Jay and me until the trial was over.

Instead, I suggested we rent us a place for the duration of the case. A place we could share that was safe and peaceful for her kids. I even made the deal sweeter; I was willing to pay for this new adventure. She agreed with the plan but decided it was only right that Kyle foot the bill. She said his funds might be a little shaky after he hires a new lawyer and finds a bail bond agent to get him out. "So you just gone leave him high and dry like that?" I asked. I was in disbelief. I mean, don't get me wrong I understood why she was doing this, but at the same time, he was like a brother to me. I told her you don't worry about anything.

I text Jay and told him to find a lawyer to bail Kyle out. I also told him I was going on a trip for a while. He was a little salty, but he understood under these circumstances. Tyesha needed me. I don't know why she decided to represent this girl, but I must go through this with her. I let her know I would be waiting for her in the car. She didn't want me to wait. She said it was best to have her assistant find a spot to rent that could house the kids and us. She didn't know how long we would need the housing, but the kids were coming back from school in the next few months. I had to give her credit for planning. We decided it was best for me to head home and pack my stuff. She would send the details once she was home.

I took a detour on my way home. I wanted to stop by and talk to Roe. Plus, I hadn't seen my beautiful nephew in about two weeks. I loved me some him. His daddy is some mystery guy Roe won't reveal. We told her she was petty as hell, and eventually, she would have to face Emjay and explain it to him when he gets older. That conversation was not going to be a good one. Hell, she knew what it felt like not to have that father figure consistently. She should never stand in the way of her child having a healthy relationship with his father. We can't tell her anything. She is one of those people

Within 20 minutes, I was pulling up to Roe's place. I always loved coming over here. Her house was so well maintained. She lived in a large townhouse. It was our first fixer upper. She had gotten pregnant seven years ago and wanted her own space. We renovated the townhouse from top to bottom. It was beautiful inside. Her favorite color was purple, and she let it be known. She would try to choose light or dark colors to match it. Now that I think about it, we all loved purple. That was something we all shared.

I parked in her garage and let myself in. I also had a key to her place. As soon as I turned the knob, I could hear moaning coming from the kitchen. I called Roe's name before I took another step. She didn't respond, so I keep walking until I reached the kitchen. Roe was sitting on the kitchen counter spread eagle with her vibrator. "Roe! You nasty as hell!" I yelled, scaring her half to death. She almost fell off the counter. I couldn't do anything but turn my face up and laugh at her pitiful attempt to reach her climax. She was embarrassed as hell. I had caught her red-handed. She wouldn't even make eye contact with me. So, I made things worse. "So, what if I was MJ coming home and you in here stroking your cat?" I asked, laughing so hard I had to wipe my tears.

"Why are you here? My child is not expected home until next Friday. I told you his school went to China for a week." Roe was gathering her clothing that had been folded on the countertop. She snatched her leggings and started to slip them on. "Make sure you clean that counter too." I said. I knew I was pissing her off. I didn't care. She was nasty for letting me walk in like this. "Who invited you in the first place. I had my plans today." Roe was essentially blaming me for not calling before I came over. I walked away from her and sat down on her purple and black leather couch. I figured I'd give her some space to get herself together. I was still having a little chuckle about the entire situation. I guess you must get it how you live.

"I needed to talk to you about this Kyle and Jay situation." I figured I would change the subject and get back to the reason I was over here. I wasn't planning on staying long, but I needed to get the scoop and compare notes. A few minutes passed, and she hadn't responded, but I could hear her footsteps approaching. Before I knew it, she had changed clothes altogether and plopped down in the reclining chair, ready to chat. "Hey, girl." She said, smiling from ear to ear. "Let's just start over." She suggested, and we both shook our heads in agreeance.

"Aight so apparently, things are pretty serious with this upcoming situation. I hate to say this, but I think Jay was involved, or he knows what's going on." She was her usual self. She thinks she is Sherlock Holmes or somebody. Leave it to Roe to crack the case and do her best to convince people her theory is correct. I was coming to my conclusions about this situation, and I was starting to think coming over here was a mistake. I wanted to tell her about the cell phone and matchbook I found. I was going to give her time to discuss her theories. I tuned in and out as she gave her a dramatic response. I would chime in with an occasional head nod the same as it would be if we were on face time.

It was finally my turn, and I stood heading towards the kitchen for some wine. "Jay is cheating on me." I said without emotions. My voice trailed off a bit as I reached the kitchen. I return in a matter of minutes after I helped myself to a glass. I sat back down graciously and took a sip of my wine. My sister was in aww, which didn't happen often. She even wore a look of worry on her face. "What's wrong with you?" I asked. She didn't respond verbally; she just shook her head and took out her cell phone. Her reaction was a bit odd, but I guess she is in just as much shock as I was. "I know you in shock, Roe, but I can prove it." I said, feeling confident. She leaned in and put her hand on my knee. "Listen, I.. I'm sorry." She said as a tear began to release from her brown eyes. She held her head down low and began to have a silent weep.

I was starting to rethink my own emotions. I hadn't even shed a tear yet. I wondered why. Why am I not as angry as Roe? I guess I am to the point where I have more important things to worry about in life. He is doing something. More importantly, he may have done something horrific. Which is why I am here. I allowed her to continue her session of weeping, and I needed to get back to the house. She finally lifted her head and said she would walk me out the door. I was in my world at this point. I couldn't understand why she was so upset. It was seriously on my mind heavy. I didn't even remember walking out to the car and cranking up. I sat there just in a daze. When you have a twin, you feel things. I hadn't had this feeling in a while, but sometimes it can be overwhelming.

I knew she was hurting. Deeply. I just couldn't figure out why I wasn't. I took the long way back to my house. I just wanted to clear my mind and gather my thoughts. I added ten minutes to my ride, but it was worth it. I was in no rush. I knew it would take a while for Tyesha to be ready for our mini hideout. The great thing was I had time to comb through everything with a clear mind while Ty could keep me updated with things from her end. When I got home, Jay was there. Today was unusual. He told me he would be working late. I pulled up and parked. I gathered all my things and headed in the house.

I dropped my bag on the wooden stand as I locked the door. The alarm didn't go off; it just chimed, letting it be known the front door opened. I kicked off my shoes. I hadn't been out for long, but it wore me the heck out. I walked upstairs slowly and began to think about what I needed to pack. I had finally made it to my bedroom, the door was opened, and Jay was sitting on his side of the bed. His eyes were red. I could tell something was up. He turned and looked at me as I entered the room. "Hey." I said. I wasn't too excited to see him this time. I had mixed feelings about him too. "Baby, don't you look beautiful?" He said.

"We need to talk." I said as I sat down beside him. I looked him in the eye and asked him what happened the night he went out with Kyle. His eyes lit up as if he was thrown off guard. As if he didn't expect me to know anything about that evening. I wonder what else he thought I was going to say. Jay shook his head and began to tell me his side of things. Of course, he denied everything. He said he was working late and they called to get into something. He agreed to go, and they were all having a good time. He claims he left and Kyle called him and told him about the situation. I never had any reason to doubt anything he ever said to me. I actually couldn't believe we were in this situation. We had been together a lifetime.

I had to be honest. As he was explaining his side of things, I chuckled, knowing that he had no idea I was going to take his ass through the wringer when this was all said and done. I suppose I should have known he could pull this off. He was running for Mayor for Christ sakes. I had no words for him. I got up from the bed and walked over to the closet. I pulled down my luggage from the top shelves. As I began pulling out some comfortable things I would like to wear, Jay came to the closet and began to plead his case. I turned and asked him what he thought I would ask him.

He hung his head low. This time he dropped to his knees. "Promise me that you will be understanding." He said. At this point, I was going to lose my mind. "Come on, Jay. Say what you need to say. I have to go." I told him. I know he could hear the frustration in my voice. Today had turned out to be a bit too much for me. I slept with his ass today, and here he is out raping people. I was starting to feel that rage that Roe began to display. I looked down at him and pushed him out the way. He was taking entirely too long to say what was on his chest. I simply continued packing my bag, deciding to go with a larger suitcase. I was starting to see why Ty wanted that getaway.

It was clear neither of us could trust the men we were madly in love with. I grabbed a few more dresses and sandals I could slip into at short notice. I also had a hunch to pack a few all-black items just in case we had to do a stakeout. I was down to ride with Ty. When its all said and done, I am hoping we all can walk away from this without any scars. For right now, I will remain optimistic and continue telling myself I am going to support Tyesha. This is not about Jay and I. Jay continued to sit on the closet floor. Weeping. I found it unusual, but I continued to bite my tongue. The proof is in the pudding. Time will tell the truth.

Minutes later, my phone was going off with a text from Tyesha. She had found a nice spot for us to lay low, and she told me to bring my bathing suit. Who could turn down a trip with water? Not I, I thought as I reached in my dresser drawer and dumped the entire stock of bathing suits in my suitcase. I was almost packed and ready to blow this joint. It didn't take long before I was leaving the house. Some reason I felt like things were about to be shaken up and stirred a bit. I don't know why I had that feeling, but it was not going to be the same. Something happened. I thank God I had a best friend who will give me front row seats to this situation.

I was out the door. I left behind a man who was sulking in his guilt. I sat my phone in its holder and synced it to the car. As I pulled out, I noticed Jay was standing at the door. I hesitated for a moment, hoping he would find the courage and run out there to stop me from leaving. I wanted him to say baby I dropped the ball on this one. I needed him not to treat me as a wife of a politician. I took a picture of the matchbook and left it exactly where I had found it. Eventually, he will see I may know more than what he thinks.

I turned on some good jams and got into a vibe. I know one thing was for sure. I needed this space. I don't want to be one of those women who get all rowdy when their man cheats. I'd rather weigh my options and make the best decision. Am I wrong for that? Does it scream to the world that I allow my husband to treat me with a lack of respect? Women are always put in a tough situation where they have to make tough decisions. I guess, for now, I will be the woman who must get her hands dirty to get the truth. I just ask that God give me the strength to deal with what will be brought to the light. Maybe by then, I will be ready with my next steps.

Chapter 2- Rolinda

Growing up with a twin was a totally different experience than just having brothers and sisters. When you are a twin you connect with them as if it was, you're connecting with yourself. It sounds weird I'm sure, but its one of the greatest experiences ever. Sure, it has its pros and cons, but reality was I did love her and slightly envied the life she built. We both had to work hard for everything we have but she literally quit her job to be a wife. I would never be that lucky. Instead, I was stuck being an entrepreneur and chasing the bag. I had a child of course out of wedlock, but I have done my best to play the role of mom and dad. Talinda never had to worry about that. She had a full scholarship and did absolutely nothing with it.

I don't want to sound like a hater, but things were just different for me. I was sitting in the living room still feeling like a bag of crap once Talinda left. As kids I could always feel her pain and vice versa. She told me that Jay was cheating on her. There were no emotions behind it. There where a few things I wanted to tell her but I didn't really know how much she knew. I broke down. I was distraught. I'm not sure which part hurt worse. I had a lot to tell Tati and I knew it was not the right time. I figured I would keep quiet and let her get her feelings off her chest. Instead she stared at me as I was obviously more upset than she was. I reacted before I could even process what she was saying. I know she knows something is up. She didn't respond. She simply walked away.

I had no energy to even chase behind her. It had been at least an hour and she still hadn't checked in on me. I couldn't sit and just wait for her to start putting things together. I finally got myself to a point where I could head to take a shower. I had an appointment with a client a little later. In my world my money comes first. Well, of course MJ will always be my number one, but mommy must make coins to give him a good life. I use to be a paralegal even though I was granted rights to practice law. I ended up investing in a business last year when I was on vacation. I ended up in Bora Bora after a bad break up and MJ spent the summer abroad in camp.

I met a group of women who were also on a personal spiritual cleanse from men and their lies. Apparently, two of the four women were owners of a very exclusive company that provided special services to the rich and wealthy. I was very intrigued and decided to set up a meeting with them. It was more so how I could be of service to them. You should never convince someone to need you. You must let them know why they will not make it without you. Within months of meeting them I was hired as their entertainment lawyer so to speak. Ever since then we have been inseparable. I enjoy the kind of work I do for them. I can assist them with keeping things in line. I can also participate in company activities. I like to call it volunteer work.

Tonight, wasn't any different. I had a dinner meeting with a potential client. I was responsible for making sure each client signed the appropriate documentation along with understanding the rules. Because our company only handled an elite group of people, we needed to make sure privacy was our number one concern. It wouldn't take long before I was heading out the door and off to make money. Tati and Jay would have to be on hold for a little while.

Within the next hour I was in my truck heading to meet my client. Whoever this client was, wanted to meet in a secure location. We had to change locations three times for some reason, so we decided on a newly built hotel on the outskirts of the city. We were surrounded by nothing but land and nature. I was starting to get a little apprehensive. I pulled up to the hotel and my client was right. No one was here. There was a limo parked in the front of the hotel by the registration entry. I parked my truck as close as I could to the building. I pinged my location to my sons email address just in case I didn't make it out of here.

I flipped down my sun visor and checked my make up to make sure I was still on point. In the business that I was in, sexiness was more than a requirement. It was a lifestyle. I got out the car and headed into the hotel. The doors opened and I walked through the glass doors. I was greeted by a waitress who offered to take my coat as she handed me a glass of Champaign and a note card. I thanked the waitress and kept my purse on me. I continued walking as I opened the note card. It read "FL2001" with an arrow pointing towards the elevator.

"Whoever the architect of this property is, is simply divine." I said as I looked back to the waitress who was no longer there. Where in the hell did she go? I let my thoughts carry me onto the elevator. I selected the last floor and held my breathe until I reached the top. This place was beautiful. The elevator was glass and it felt like I was floating. Finally, the doors chimed, and I had reached my destination. I walked around the entire floor looking for 2001. There was no other direction on my note card. I stood there admiring the view of the city. The lights in the evening time were stunning. As I continued to wait I was taken off guard by a gentleman.

He was fine as hell. I stood about 6'4 caramel skin. He was wearing a fitted grey suite with some nice brown dress shoes. He was sharp. He held out his hand to introduce himself. "Hello, I'm Rico." He said in a deep baritone voice. I cleared my voice before I replied. I had given him a fake name. In my line of business, I never disclose my identity. "I'm Tiffany." I said bashing my eyes. "So, shall we get started?" I asked. He led the way to glass door that I had no idea was even there. It opened to the lounge area where there was a waiter and waitress waiting to assist us. The view in this area was magnificent. As we approached the tables, we were handed a one page menu.

Things were moving slowly; I was ready to get to the point of this meeting. I didn't want to rush it but I needed to get to the point. We sat and talked over a three-course meal. I finally presented him with the paperwork needed to be allowed to attend our events. Rico noticed I pulled out the documents and he took another sip of his drink. He wiped his mouth and hands before reaching for his pen. "You know, I don't know if I really need to sign these papers." He said as he read over the first two pages. "I wanted to hire your company for something else." He said. I was totally intrigued by this time.

Depending on what he is needing my night may be ending soon. "I need to know if my request will be safe." He said all suspiciously. I nodded my head in agreeance because I had to know what he wanted. "I represent some powerful people who may want a little fun soon. I wanted to know if it was possible to bring the party to us. We have a lot of events in which we need to keep people occupied." He paused for a second to study my face. I held out my hand letting him know it was ok to continue. I had seen it all in my line of work. Hell my twin sister walked in on me earlier getting my rocks off on the counter. I was in no mood to judge him.

Rico continued, "to be honest I know the owner of the company and with all the new policies now she is requesting that I meet with you. I have received the approval already on the back end. I just need the paperwork for legal purposes." I was floored. There was obviously no point of me being here. I did my best to contain my facial expression. " Well Rico, if you all are all squared away just send me a list of expectations and I will get back to you with the proper paperwork" I placed my napkin on the table and begin to rise to head out. "Wait!" He said as I had turned to leave the room. "I have something else I wanted to talk to you about." He said.

I turned back around and sat down silently. I continued to listen to his issue. He did his best to leave out names but apparently the woman Kyle was being accused of raping is an employee on the job. I didn't know what to say. His version of things makes it out to be more than just Kyle. I told him I would get back to him on whether I was willing to help on this case. Before I could reach the elevator, he hollered out to me. "It's your job. You have no choice in this matter." His voice echoed through the empty floor. I didn't respond, there was no need to do so. The elevator was there to take me back down to the lobby.

Who in the hell was this Rico dude for him to know what my job is? I hadn't heard of him before today. I had a few things that I needed to follow up on. First things first. I was going to reach out to the two owners I had invested with. I know I was responsible to represent the company and those who are employed. However, I keep a log of events and there was nothing scheduled for that week. There must be other services that we offer that I don't know about. I was in my car searching for a group chat option in my phone. I was slightly pissed because they could have warned me about this meeting today. Before pulling off I sent a text out.

As I was pulling off, I saw Mr. Rico getting into his limo. I rolled my eyes as I turned the corner. He was so arrogant. Nonetheless, I needed to head back to the office and do some work. Clearly, I was now responsible for getting a settlement on this case with this mysterious girl. How in the heck did I even get involved with this? I wanted to tell Tati so bad, but I know she has a lot on her plate right now. Before I could even think of what and how I was going to pull this off my phone was ringing. I pressed the green phone button on my steering wheel. "Talk to me." I said as I looked over to the screen to see who was calling.

"Hey it's Nina." She was the owner of the company I worked for. "Hey girl. What's going on?" I asked as I was jumping on the highway headed towards the office. "Nothing much, how was the meeting?" She asked. I had a feeling she already knew how it went. "I'm not really sure. So, what is really going on with this rape situation?" I asked. It was no need to play I jumped straight to it. She hesitated before she spoke. "Meet me at the office. We need to talk but not over the phone. "Her tone was so serious. I knew things may be worse than what we knew. I told her I was headed to the office right now and that it was a perfect time to meet. She agreed.

We said our goodbyes and I was arriving to our office. It was perfect timing. I went into the parking deck and sat in the car for a few more minutes. I had a thing where before I meet with anyone, I keep a log. I had a bad experience before, so I must make sure I write down everything. I pulled out my planner and made a few notes. Before I got out the car I checked my surroundings and exited the vehicle. I continued to look around to make sure no one else was on this floor. I reached the elevator still looking around. As I entered the elevator I saw a familiar black car pulling up. I quickly pressed the button to my destination. I wonder who else was coming into the office? Within a few seconds I was exiting the elevator and heading to my office. Security was sitting at the desk monitoring the cameras.

I spoke and continued to my safe space. I needed to look at a few files to see what I could find on this Rico fellow. I also needed to get into my computer. We are no longer allowed to take home any equipment from work. I had to enforce that rule once I came on. I heard about a few events that happened last year and security breach was the main cause. Sometimes I hated we had the rule because it makes things so difficult in times such as these. I scanned my hand to unlock my office door and kicked my shoes off before sitting down.

I pressed play on my speaker and allowed smooth Jazz to get me in the zone. I cracked open my laptop and got to work. Before I knew it, two hours had passed, and there was a knock on my door. I glanced at the camera to see who it was before allowing them to enter. It was Nina, and she was talking to someone else that was outside of the camera's view. I hit the button to slide the doors back so they could enter. My face must have been telling them what I was thinking. Nina immediately started to introduce the crew as they all walked into my office.

"Good evening Roe. I brought a few people with me." Nina said as she had wholly entered. I nodded my head, letting her know it was ok to come. Before she could say anything else, I stood and motioned for everyone to leave my office and follow me to the conference room. My office was large but not large enough for two big burly men, Nina and myself. Among those men, I noticed a familiar face. It was Mr. Rico from earlier. I had no idea he would be here. At this point, I am learning to expect nothing and accept everything.

Once we reached the conference room, I scanned my hand to enter. We all found a seat around the glass bench and put our eyes towards the front. Nina fell right into place. She should have known this was a conversation for much more extensive accommodation. Nina stood in the front of the room, thanking us all for coming out tonight. She said she wanted to discuss a few things tonight, one of which being this very sticky situation in which we are unable to leave the building without a plan. From that point, she pressed the intercom on the wall behind her. "Jodi, could you order some dinner, please. It's a group of five." She ordered. She then turned to us and continued.

"Last year, we had a few situations that we handled. This year it's clear we are going to have to battle another storm. I like the fact we are here tonight. It lets me know I have a hell of a team. As I stated earlier tonight, we are sharing this room with myself, Rolinda, Jerry, Rico, and Tae. We all handle a specific portion of this company that helps it all operate. We had an incident with a few of Tae's girls. There were a total of four females involved in this unfortunate incident. What the police don't know is there were only three females listed on the report. One of the girls lost their life that night, and it is our responsibility to get to the bottom of it.

From my understanding, one of the ladies has quit and decided to seek counsel elsewhere." She paused for a moment wanting to give us a second to allow it to sink in. She continued once making eye contact with everyone in the room. "One of the people who are responsible for this attack is also a client of ours. He is running for Mayor. We must decide if we will stand behind the victim or if we shall stand behind our client. We all will have mixed decisions.

Now, I have prepared a presentation that will review both cases with true and real facts. We must be careful with how we handle this. We don't want to send the message to our clients that their confidentiality is at risk yet again. We also don't want to show our wonderful employees we don't have their backs. This is a tough situation. I will sit down and play the presentation. Are there any questions at this time?" she asked. Nina was a boss, and she conducted herself with so much confidence.

She was right; this was a significant decision. Rico is responsible for exclusive clients, and he believes I should support the upcoming mayor. Tae was here to defend her girls. Someone needed to pay for the murder of her worker. Jerry, he was here because he ran numbers.

He needed to be there to ensure we don't lose. We must make the best decision for the company. No one had any questions, so Nina walked away from the front and headed to take a seat. She pulled a remote control for the screen out of the glass bar drawer. I hopped up and asked if anyone wanted something to drink before we got started. I took drink orders and left the room for a few minutes. My mind was racing; I couldn't believe we were in this situation. The decision will be tough. I don't want to make assumptions, but I only know of one person that runs around with Kyle.

I never knew Sonjay was a client of ours. I quickly rushed into my office and opened my laptop. I accessed our client list and searched for Sonjay's name. There it was clear as day. His pin name was Tati's birthday. I was so pissed. How could he do this to me, and Tati? I was so close to another breakdown, but I had to shake it off.

Sonjay had a lot of explaining to do. This whole situation is messy. I knew I had to get back to the conference room, so I grabbed a pen and tablet to write on. I stopped by the breakroom and grabbed a few things out of the fridge. When I returned, our food was delivered. It was Italian, which was my favorite. Rico held the door open for me as I tried to get past him to distribute the drinks. "Excuse me, Miss Rolinda," he said, putting extra emphasis on my name. I felt terrible, but in this business, I couldn't share certain things with him.

I laughed off his comment. I knew he would make it out. Besides, he didn't need to know my name, anyway. He and Nina are a thing. I can't say I am mad at that though. He is fine as ever. I wonder if he had a brother or something I could meet. My thoughts pondered off as Nina brought the attention back to the front of the room. "Alright guys, now that we are all back, we will start the presentation. Does anyone have any objections to dimming the lights?" She asked. No one answered. She finally pressed play and sat down. I began to eat my food and watch the presentation. I took notes as much as I could.

Nina made it clear we could not leave here without a solid plan. Two hours had gone past as we all were looking dead. Nina hit the lights, making us all sit up. I checked my watch, and it was one in the morning. It was super late, and we were all tired. This presentation was intense. I was right the mayor; Nina was referring to was indeed Sonjay. Kyle was not a member of El Fetche, but due to his association with Jay, he was able to get into all the parties as a plus one. They had both been attending El Fetche's events for a long time. Nina showed us footage of the last two events they participated in together. It appears things were escalating. Tae begins to speak up once the lights were on. She got up and stood in front of the room.

"I know it is late and we are all ready to go. I think we need a break. I ask that you all stand and stretch while I shed some light on a few things. Once done discussing, take a few minutes to use the restroom, and when you return, we will continue the presentation. We all did as we were requested. We stood and began to stretch. You could hear everyone's bones cracking. We were all fly as hell on the outside, but the reality was, we were old. We all chuckled as we could hear our bones about to break. Tae begins talking as she started to do squats.

"I want to clear a few things up. This presentation is amazing, but it doesn't say everything. I am responsible for private events that not listed on the books. I uphold my schedule. I frequently book exclusive clients that work with Rico. In this situation, the running mayor, Mr. Sonjay Boyd, got his common room and was accompanied by Kyle McNeil, who is his campaign manager. They had a few others with them who all wanted to have a good time. According to one of the girls not listed in these allegations,

Sonjay was responsible for the murder of one of my girls. She said they discussed calling us to resolve the issue. In this discussion, they decided if anyone took the fall, it would be the two college friends. However, Kyle's name ended up being the only one listed. As for the dearly departed, Ashley Toliver's remains are in the dumpster five blocks from the hotel. Her family has not yet reported her missing." Once Tae was finished with her last hamstring stretch, she walked back over to her seat. No one said anything.

I cleared my throat and opened the floor up for a bathroom break, and asked if anyone had any questions. This room was full of tension. It was almost like we were all dying to scream. All you could hear in the room were papers shuffling. We were jotting down notes and rereading what we had previously written. I sent a text to Nina, letting her know I was going to light a joint in this office to ease the tension. I also told her that I was still unsure who I think we should stand behind. She wrote back, giving me the heads up that it was ok to light up. We try to keep certain practices out of the office when we have company. The reality was, she didn't have to threaten me with a good time. It took me little to no time to pull out my pre-rolled lifesaver.

Nina brought the attention back to the front of the room. She was ready to hit continue on the presentation. Before she began, she gave another disclaimer. "This part of the presentation will show something the police have no record of knowing. This situation is where things get real. As stakeholders in this company, this is what is going to make or break your decision. I want you to look at the footage that was captured by one of the ladies on their cell phones." The room fell quiet again, so I lit up the peacemaker. Nine removed herself from the front and pressed play.

The room was pitch black for a second, and all you could hear was noises. It sounded like someone was moaning. Then you could listen to someone arguing about money. It was one of the girls asking for her pay so she could leave. Her asking this is unorthodox because we never allow them to pay our girls. We are not running a prostitution ring. Now, if things happen to escalate and sexual favors exchanged between two consenting adults, that is their business. El Fetche handles the undesirables for our clients. We also own a private division that allows our girls to be dates for the evening or help the party look full by suppling a few models for the evening.

I had to admit I was disappointed when I heard it. I made a note to make sure I discuss this with Tae. Our clients can tip, but they are not allowed to make new deals without our knowledge. As the tape continued to play, we could hear glass breaking, and then we saw an image we never thought we would see. It was Sonjay on top of this defenseless woman raping her while strangling her. Her moans went from pleasure to terror. We stared at the screen; Sonjay displayed his rage and frustration, taking it out on this poor girl. Kyle was at the table with a female on her knees. He sat there and watched Sonjay lose control.

Tears began to roll down my eyes. This was worse than I thought. The first part of this presentation was factual and about the history of Sonjay's history here as a client. He did kill her. I cannot believe he killed her. I had never seen him so enraged. It's hard to fathom that my sister is dating a murderer. How could we have missed this? I had personally only heard him raise his voice once since I have known him. It was clear what I needed to do. My heart was saying I should call my sister and tell her everything. That would put my job here in jeopardy. On the other hand, I was breaking on the inside, just thinking of him harming someone, let alone a woman. How did we get here?

My thoughts had taken me away from the presentation at this moment. I hadn't noticed my silent tears had turned into sobbing. As I took one last pull on the peacemaker before passing it to Rico, I noticed everyone was looking at me. I had interrupted the presentation and hadn't noticed. Nina was rubbing my back and giving me tissues. Rico took the peacemaker out of my hand, and I apologized to the group. Tae then stood up and asked if I needed excusing? She admitted it was difficult to watch but also stated how important it was to get through this.

I nodded my head in agreeance. I motioned for them to continue. I had so many emotions running through me at the moment, but I had a job to do. Nina pressed play again. The video continued. Ashley's body laid there lifeless as the cameraman started to adjust themselves to get closer. Her eyes connected with ours. They were hazel; the room was quiet on both ends of the monitor. We were speechless as we watched Sonjay unpeel himself from her corpse. Kyle finally stood up and looked over at the other people in the room.

He noticed the camera was on and lost it. "Shut it down now!" he screamed, walking towards the camera person. They kept it on. He tried to knock the camera out of their hands, and he still didn't get it. Sonjay was heading over to join Kyle in confiscating the phone. The other people in the room sat in the corner, shaking. Shortly after, we could see the phone knocked on the ground, and you caught a glimpse of them kicking the cameraman. Kyle unzipped his pants and proceeded to "give her what she was asking for." Before the camera turned off, Sonjay was inserting himself in her rear end. She was screaming so loudly. They both mutilated the poor girl.

The video ended, and the screen rolled back up into the ceiling. The lights remained off, and the room was dead silent. I lit another peacemaker in the dark. We still sat there. No one knew what to say. Where do we even begin? It was clear; El Fetche could not support Sonjay and Kyle. We must take up for Ashley and the other women involved in this incident. My mind was racing, and I had no idea what I was going to do. There were so many elements to this. I took long, deep pulls off the peacemaker. I choked on the last pull, so I passed it to Rico. It was so hard to see in the dark. I asked Nina to hit the light. Seconds later, we shared a laugh as I tried to explain how I couldn't see.

Nina decided to open the floor up while we enjoyed our smoking session. She reached out to the intercom and asked Jodi to bring in some munchie foods so we could get through the rest of the meeting. We hadn't heard from a few people in the room tonight, so it was time to listen to what they had to say. Rico decided to speak his mind. I had to admit, he could say anything to me, and I would buy into it. His voice was baritone, almost like Barry White. He spoke with such conviction. I only wish I could have a man so strong and powerful.

The men I always fall for are the ones already taken. I allowed my eyes to undress him as he stood in front of the room. He began to speak, and I was still staring at his unmentionables, and I think Nina started to notice. She cleared her throat, interrupting him a tad. I, of course, snapped out of my trance. Rico began to speak once more. "Ok, this was a lot to take in. I know we all won't do the right thing here." He paused for a moment. Then he continued. "My first instinct is to, of course, stand behind our ladies. Without them, we would not function. I want them to feel protected while employed with El Fetche." He paused again, and this time before he spoke, he leaned down and took a deep breath. "Here is where things get hard." "I think we also have to put a few things out there. Protecting our clientele is what we do. Were they wrong? Hell yeah. What happened was horrible. We should allow the police to handle the prosecution."

"So, where does that leave us?" He asked, looking around the room. "I think that leaves us exposed. For us to make money, we have to have our clientele protected at all times. Is there anything we can do to hide the fact the women worked for us, and the men took advantage of them. I think we should stand behind our clients to bury any association with El Fetche." He had finished his little speech, and I can't say that I was too pleased.

Nina thanked him for the feedback and called up the accountant, Jerry. He looked shocked to be called up to the front to shed some light on how this could affect us financially. Jerry was a weird character. You would think he was a bodyguard, but once you got to know him, you would know he was a gentle soul. He cleared his throat, but before he could speak, Jodi was coming through the door with snacks. She was right on time; we all had enjoyed a piece of a peacemaker. We needed some tasty refreshments. As she sat the bags on the table, we all crowded around her like savages.

"Oh, Jodi. Thank you so much! She had gone to my favorite chicken spot. She brought back the works: chips, chocolates, and soda. I could kiss her right now for this goodness. We all started to dig in. Poor Jerry stood in the front of the room, sucking the gristle off the leg. He tossed it in the trash next to him and licked his fingers. He then began to speak. "Well, tonight has been eventful. He flashed us all with a huge smile. I can also agree- I think what has happened to our girls is devastating, and we should be doing better to protect them. Now that we have that established, neither side would win financially." He paused, allowing it to sink in.

We all looked at each other. I don't know if it was horror or confusion, but either way, we were worried. "If you choose to go with supporting the ladies, there will be extensive training that needs to take place; we would need to bring El Fetche to the light publicly. That alone will run away our clientele. Supporting the gentlemen would be just as bad. We would be providing our clients the power to get out of control without consequences." He paused for a second and then told us that was all he had. "The input was useful, but it doesn't get us any closer to a resolution. Nina still hadn't given her opinion. Tae spoke earlier, but she has headed to the front anyways.

"I will make this quick. I think we should stand behind our ladies', no questions asked. It may cost money to train them on self-defense and to improve our policies, but I'd prefer to do that a thousand times over than to allow another man to cause harm." Her tone sounded broken, and her eyes looked like she cried hard before coming to the front. She walked away from the front with her head high. She meant what she said, and I had to be honest, I agreed with her. I say no matter how hard it will be to take them down. We should do it.

Nina looked over at me, letting me know it was my turn to take the front. I nodded and made my way to the front of the room. I had no idea where to start. I could feel the layers of my blooming onion beginning to peel. I needed to sort out my thoughts, but I guess that was the point of this whole evening. I stood up front, fiddling with my hands. I was stuck, not to mention high. So I approached the room the best way I could. I went in my pouch and pulled out another peacemaker. Everyone laughed. I lit it and took a huge pull. I exhaled deeply. I began to speak; I quickly decided whatever came to mind was the choice I would stand by.

"Look, this is difficult for me to contribute my input, but it's my job." I pulled on the peacemaker once more. "I say that because I know the murderer on a personal level. I love this man; he is apart of my family. I wouldn't have my...." My voice trailed off as I needed to slow down on releasing my first thoughts. "He is married to my sister. I didn't know he was apart of the company in any way or fashion. What I do know is- he deserves everything that happens to him. I do not think El Fetche should support the client in this incident. I think we should turn this footage over to the police.

They never mention El Fetche's name in the footage. It is also a part of the contracts when accepting membership; we maintain a strict confidentiality rule. Not to mention it also states if things become drastically uncontrollable, El Fetche will assist the police department in any way, shape, or form. I do agree that we should be doing more to protect our ladies. That is something that I am for sure going to follow up on to ensure we do not have any of these incidents in the future. We also need to communicate harassment is not accepted. From a legal standpoint- I think we would be fools not to support the women." I felt a thousand times better. I needed to release that.

As I was taking a seat and notice, Tae was looking over at me. She was wearing a subtle smile on her face. I knew she understood where I was coming from about this situation. Nina was the last one to take the floor. She looked stressed. She slowly waltzed to the front of the room. She cleared her throat and asked me if she could take a pull of the peacemaker. We all shared a laugh, and I let her hit it before she gave her opinion. "Alright, gang. I first want to say thank you for coming to make this decision tonight. This is quite a long evening. We are doing one hell of a job tonight. I guess my decision will always be to decide what is best for this company." Nina started to pace around the room, but it was helping her to process her thoughts.

"I started this company many years ago with three out of the five of us in this room. It was the best time of my life. I have been close to losing this place just last year. Yet here I am now facing another challenge. Does this make me want to fold? Tuh, yea. I want to bury my head in my pillows right now." We all laughed. She was doing what she does best, bringing things back into perspective. "I think we continue to survive because of our fight and our values. I think I agree with Rolinda.

I think we should honor our handbook and current policy and procedures we currently have. I am very interested in developing our employees more. I think we could see those expenses as well needed. I think we should stand behind our ladies here in El Fetche. What they did was wrong. Thank goodness all of them weren't hurt beyond repair. We should disassociate ourselves with the gentlemen." Her tone was serious.

She wanted to remove them from any association with El Fetche. This could work, to be honest. Sending notification to Sonjay can let him know we are not backing him, yet his contract on confidentiality still stands. Nina may be on to something. I am hoping we can all agree on this. "So, now that everyone has said their piece, what do we do?" I asked, getting straight to the point. We all looked around and didn't speak. I continued. "I hate this decision as much as you all do.

But it has to be made. Raise your hand if you want to support the women." I wrote down the number of hands I saw. "Okay, now tell me who would like to support the clients in this situation." I looked around once more and jotted down the number of hands that were up. I then looked at the paper I was holding.

I slid it over to Nina. We all could count, and the rules have always been majority rules. Either way, I am sure we will get backlash. I will start preparing for litigation just in case we happen to come up in the investigation. Nina stood one last time thanking us for being here and that we were all free to leave now that we had a decision. I was no longer tired. Besides, I doubt I will be getting any sleep in the upcoming weeks. I had a lot to do to protect this company but, more importantly, my sister and myself. Once I walk out of this office, I know that things will not be the same. I already know Tati will disown me if I bring this to her. I have no idea what Ty has been able to find out on her end, but it was clear we could make this situation better or worse. Nothing in between.

Things will be interesting for a while, but I honestly think we are making the right decision despite what we feel. I had to be honest with myself and with Nina. This was not going to be an easy task. We needed to stay grounded and away from any media. I also warned her that all parties would receive some kind of communication to eliminate any involving's of El Fetche. It was clear, with everything we have seen and heard today both parties violated the by-laws of El Fetche. I will review the contracts to see if there were any loopholes, that was for sure.

We all dispersed after being dismissed. I went back to my office to do some digging. It was so much I found out while watching the presentation. I needed a moment to myself to review my files. There was so much to dive into that I needed to fully process to make sure any decisions we made were the best for all parties but especially El Fetche. I think there was more to the story.

Chapter 3: Ty and Tati

It was a bittersweet moment to see my husband hauled off in the back of the Sheriff's car. I wanted to tell him so badly, but I knew I couldn't blur those lines. I tried talking to him when he got home, but he couldn't keep up with the conversation. Before I could drop any hints to his ignorant ass, we had a knock on the door. The look in his eyes let me know he was guilty. It was like he expected it. I couldn't say anything for the most part. He assumed I would be his lawyer because usually, that is how things went. In this case, I knew I couldn't bail my husband out. I was going to be the opposing lawyer. I knew this would alter my relationship, but am I not supposed to do the right thing?

I told Tati I was going away for a bit until all of the dust settles. She agreed to come with me being as though Sonjay may be involved. Sonjay has a lot of things going for himself. I have no idea what he was thinking about getting involved with Kyle and his shenanigans? I had my assistant from the office to remove all my meetings for the next month. I advised they would have to be virtual meetings and asked for her to find someone else to take over a few of my cases. I did let her know I am not shutting down all the way, but I needed to focus on this case at hand. She is delivering all of the case files to the property. It should be no longer than an hour's drive away from the city.

From my understanding, it would be a beautiful set up that will allow us to focus without any distractions. She sent me an email with all of the details of the rental property. I had to admit she found something rather quickly, but it was beautiful. It was a clay house, the ones built to keep out the heat. It had a beautiful pool with an outdoor bar. I couldn't wait to be able to take a dip in the pool. I hit up Tati and sent her the details. I had finished packing, and I looked myself in the mirror one last time before I left. When I locked the door, I turned and paused for a moment. This may be the last time I come to this home. I don't want it to be, but, hopefully, by me having a front-row seat to all the case files will exonerate him.

I trust my client because, by law, I have to make sure there is a fair trial. I will do my best to make sure things are processed fairly. It will be difficult; I can't say that it will not be. I pray the good Lord gives me the strength. I started the ignition and connected the Bluetooth, "Hey Siri- play my riding songs." I was ready to rock out. I looked in my purse as I slowly edged out of my driveway. I rambled around until I found my treats. Heck, I may be a lawyer, but I still liked to get high. I refused to smoke it for the most part. Right now, it is a special occasion. I pulled out a nice joint as I like it and lit it up.

I turned opposite of what my GPS instructed me to do. I wanted to take the long way to the rental property. I needed this drive more than ever. I couldn't even hop on the highway before my phone began to buzz. I instructed Siri to answer the line. My music went on pause, and I answered. "This is Tyesha," I said. The caller was unknown, so I had to be professional when I picked up. "You have received a call from Kyle at the California State Prison.

If you would like to accept this call, please press 1." The automated system allowed me time to press 1. I am not sure what type of face I was making at this point. I couldn't lie. Did I want to take this call? Heck no. I was so pissed to even be in this situation. But, until he is proven guilty, I guess I need to give him the benefit of the doubt. I took a long pull off of my joint and exhaled as the operator connected Kyle.

"Baby? Can you hear me?" I heard his voice, and I knew he was distraught. Reluctantly I answered. "I'm here, Kyle. The question is, have you figured out why you are there?" I asked. I was petty, and maybe now was not the time, but he needed to know I was more than angry. I was hurt. "Yeah, they told me I am in here on some bogus rape charges. I didn't do this, Ty," he said, sounding more stressed.

The reality was setting in for him. Even if he did not do this- he was in the situation. That alone was bad enough. "I am not sure what you want me to say. I am a bit shocked." I said. Letting him know how I was feeling. He paused for a minute and began talking again. "Listen, I know things don't make sense right now, baby, I will explain everything to you. I need representation", he said, sounding like he was seemingly annoyed.

The audacity of him to think I am required to be his representation. I continued to smoke and drive. I told him that I could not represent him and he started shouting on the phone. I could feel my rage building, so I had to get off this phone call. Instead of arguing back and forth with him, I simply ended the call. What could he do? Call me back? I finished that call so quickly. I was willing to make sure he had another lawyer. When my husband gets like that, there is no talking to him. I didn't want to ruin my peaceful drive by engaging in an argument with a man who was only allowed a few minutes to talk. He better start thinking about his actions and reflect on why he is in there in the first place.

I snapped back into my peaceful trance. Siri- turn on my turn up playlist. I was in the mood at this point to listen to something with a little bounce to it. He had my blood pressure high. I continued to smoke and vibe out. I had no idea what Kyle and I will do, but all of that will be placed on the back burner until we get this case going. I already had us on the docket for first thing in the morning. It was going to be a long night. I had to prepare for the preliminary hearing. Even though I took the long route to the rental, my eta was within the next thirty minutes. I asked Siri to hit up my assistant and ask her to confirm if she had a chef for the evening. It didn't take her long to confirm the chef was already inside the home preparing a meal.

I was elated. Between my joint, good music, and a meal I can crush soon, today turned out to be alright. I had to focus on the positive. I was not going to be able to make it if I continue to think of the defendant as my husband. I must turn that switch off from here on out. They should all know from the past cases I don't play when it comes to making things happen. I took a vow to protect and serve the ones who don't have a voice. This is my job, and I won't toss it to the side because I am in my feelings. One joint turned into two. I was only a few minutes out. I didn't read the rules on their smoking policy, so I made sure my buzz would last a while.

I arrived a few moments later. The neighborhood was charming, and I didn't know this area had so many magnificent houses. I was intrigued. I would have never thought this much clear land was out here. As I drove around the subdivision, I noticed there were so many families out in their yards playing. It was beautiful to see, to be honest. The best thing about it, they were all African American or Indian.

When I was a kid, I would have never imagined seeing a sight like this. It was always something that was a figment of our imaginations. I finally pulled up to my destination. Siri chimed, letting me know I had arrived. There was a car parked in the driveway, and it was an orange Lincoln. It must be the chef's car. I sat in the car, smoking my joint, still embracing my surroundings.

It looked just like the picture. Typically properties are a little different than what they show online. So far, so good. If the inside looked like the outside, I'd say I am ahead of the game in this situation. I made a mental note that if I needed to look for a new place- I knew where I would purchase.

My joint had finally gone out, and I looked around in my purse for my body oil. I loved to partake, but I do not need anyone knowing my business. I rolled the windows down and waited a few minutes to air out. As I was gathering my items, I noticed there was a white vehicle coming up the driveway. It looked like a work van. I rolled my windows up and allowed the van to park and exit. Once he walked to the other side of the van, the door slid open and revealed case files. My documents have arrived. There was no need for me to wait any longer.

I hopped out of my truck, eager to accept his delivery. "Good evening, I can take those off your hand's sir', I said as I pulled my dolly out the back. I was always prepared. Being in my type of working environment, you can't wait for anyone to do it for you, you have to stay ready. The delivery driver flashed his pearly whites and allowed me to take the files. I had to make two trips to the steps. Once I brought back the last shipment, I unlocked the door. I made sure the delivery driver was backing out. I was a little paranoid. Netflix could have you jumping every time the wind blows with all those suspense movies I watch on it. I had to be living in a movie right now.

As he backed his white work van out of the driveway, I could see headlights of another vehicle approaching. Immediately I noticed it was Tati. She was jamming super hard. I was kind of embarrassed since we were in such a beautiful neighborhood. My delightful smile turned into a rigorous stare. She caught the drift quickly and turned her system down. I mean, I get it; I was jamming on the way here, but once you notice your surroundings, you adapt. Tati was my baby, but she lives in her world without consideration at times. No shade, though.

I patiently waited for her to gather her things and head towards the door. It only took her minutes to make it to the door, and we embraced each other as if we hadn't just seen one another. I think it was more to the hug. We both have some things on our minds, that was for sure. Nonetheless, I was ready to begin this journey of truth. No matter the outcome, I will be ok, and Tati will be ok as well. "What's all of this? I know you said it would be a while, but did you move out?" Tati finally released her embrace and looked at all the boxes we had to drag into the house.

"I have to work Tati- and you're supposed to be here to help me. Right?" I asked inadvertently. My day had been long enough. I wanted to make sure she knew this wasn't a vacation for neither of us. She looked at me and smiled. "Duh Ty, it was a joke. You need to lighten up if we are going to make this work. I know things are weird in your world and all. But it's weird for me too." Tati smiled and then told me to get the fuck out the way if I wasn't going to bring anything in the house. We shared a laugh, and I agreed to lighten up throughout the time we are here. She was right. This was not her fault, and I can't take my frustrations out on her.

It took us all of five minutes to use the dolly and drag everything, including our suitcases in the house. It was beautiful inside. It smelled like we had just walked into a Creole restaurant. It smelled amazing. Tati turned and looked at me as if someone had just rocked her world. We love food. I think tonight was going to be a good night after all. This beautiful mansion will be our new home. "Ty? Did you plan this?" She asked. "Nope," I answered. "This was all my assistant. She did an amazing job." I said. I had no right to take credit for this. I may even have to make this a thing. When I get significant cases and need some space, she can always rent me another house.

We left everything at the door and began to tour the home. We followed the smell, and it t led us to the kitchen area. We found our chef in the refrigerator bent over. I didn't want to scare him or her. I honestly couldn't tell if it was a male or female. Either way, those hips were lovely. I cleared my throat. The chef jumped and bumped their head, turning around, acknowledging someone else is in the room with her. It was a female. She was beautiful. Quite frankly, if I were a tambourine player and single, I would be happy to let her toss my salad.

My thoughts must have been written all over my face. I stood there, sizing up the chef. She was tall and chocolate, nothing I would expect a chef to be. Her hair was in a messy bun, and her skin was as smooth as a baby's bottom. Tati must have noticed I was at a loss for words. She stepped in between us and extended her hand to introduce herself. "Hi! I'm Tati. The food smells so good." Tati was a lifesaver. I needed her to rescue me from temptation. The old me would have gone with my first instinct and knocked all the food off the counter and taken her right there, but the Holy and married me, simply charmed her with my eyes.

Guilty? Not guilty? Hell, Kyle was doing him. Maybe I wouldn't be so hurt if I was doing my own thing. I finally snapped out my trance as Tati nudged me, bringing me back to life. "Um, I'm sorry. Hi, I'm Ty." I smiled nervously. She smiled again, coming in closer for a hug. "I'm Chef Royal. I hope you don't mind, and I let myself in so I could get started on dinner tonight," she said. I shook my head, letting her know I didn't mind at all. I told her we would be out of her way, and she was welcome to crash here if she needed to based on how far she lived from here.

Tati looked over at me and then back at the chef. Maybe I spoke too soon. I did sound a little thirsty. For some reason, she just made me hot and bothered. I don't know if it was the food or if it was her goddess exterior that stood in front of me. She was Creole herself. You can tell she cooked the food with her heart. It smelled like love. We wrapped up our awkward exchange and got out of her way. She said dinner would be ready in an hour or so. She had some wine chilling in all of the refrigerators throughout the house.

We both were taken aback for a second. Not only did she make sure we had chilled wine, but did she say refrigerators meaning plural? I was eager to get to the rest of the house. We saw there was an elevator in the house. Tati checked it for a weight limit, and we were good to load up some of the boxes. We reduced the load by taking four trips instead of one. As we're exiting the elevator to pull the last load of stuff, chef Royal was waiting with a tray of goodies.

"Edibles, anyone?" she asked. Tati and I both looked over at one another and giggled. "Hell yeah. What you got?" We both said in unison as we approached the tray she was holding. We were in heaven. We had so many options. We had strawberry gummy bears, green weed leaf chocolate bites, infused moon pies, and last but not least, a box with eight joints. I don't know how we found this chef, but I needed to keep her in real life. If her food is half as good as her service, I am good with that.

We stuffed a few items in our mouths while I grabbed one of the joints. "Are you familiar with this house?" I asked. I needed to know if we could smoke inside the house. "I guess you can say that. I am close to the owner," Royal said as she proceeded to take out a lighter. I wanted to know more. I allowed her to light my joint, and I followed her back to the kitchen. "Do you have anything stronger than wine?" I asked. I was about to head back upstairs and bury my head in paperwork. I needed one stiff drink to get this party started.

She quickly served me up a nice double shot of vodka. To be honest, at this point, I wanted to snatch the bottle and head upstairs, but I decided to act my age and stay in my lane. I drowned my sorrows and headed back upstairs. Tati was waiting in the same spot by the elevator. She had a look of disapproval on her face, but I hadn't done anything. The quick ride upstairs echoed with a bunch of noises from the peanut gallery. We arrived at our destination; we looked around to all of the junk we had collected, and we were not close to being unpacked by a longshot.

I decided to leave it there. Tati and I came up with a plan for the night that allowed us a few hours to sleep for a fresh start in the morning. We met in the middle of the floor, both of us taking one box each. I handed her a notepad, highlighter, and pen. I knew she would be able to help me out. If anyone would have my back, Tati would. Besides, she could have been practicing law if it wasn't for her arrogant husband. In college, we would have cram nights where we would stay up, and binge eat food until our brains were full, with both food and knowledge.

"I miss this, Tati," I said as I looked over at her. She was sitting Indian style with her reading glasses on. She was so cute sitting there with her pen hanging out of her mouth. "Don't be weird, Ty." She said, brushing me off. I didn't care whether or not if she didn't want to hear what I had to say. It was my truth. I didn't say anything else. I continued to unpack the documents stuffed in my box. I had no idea who was responsible for packing up the boxes, but they had papers that didn't make any sense.

I sat and read thoroughly through each paper. I came across a piece of paper that resembled an invoice. I laid it to the side until I could figure out what to do with it. I could discover more invoices. I continued to dig and found a photo of the plaintiff and a group of friends. I am unsure of the kind of work my client does, but the picture painted a pretty impressive image. It was clear those invoices were for paid services. I wrote a few notes down on my note pad. The filing system was great as I continued to dig into my box. I had a few piles.

Anything that had an invoice had a picture to capture the evening. So far, I hadn't found anything worth having. Suddenly, I came across a batch of room keys. They were from so many locations; there were motels to five-star hotels. I ran into a picture with some familiar faces, and my heart dropped. Something told me to see if there was a date on the image. I flipped over the picture, and it was marked eight years ago. I was shocked. I held the photo out, but I was speechless. Tati noticed my gesture and took the picture from my hands.

She looked at the photo and had the same reaction as I did. How in the hell did our husbands know this woman in college? We were all young and dumb, and the picture showed them in the school apartments off-campus. It was a picture of the boys holding a hand full of flesh. I was so pissed. I snatched a joint out and lit it up. "Do you see that?" I asked Tati as I took another pull. "Let me get this straight. Your client, is she in this picture right now?" Tati asked. She hadn't seen any photos, nor have I released her name.

"I think we are getting more than what we bargained for," I said. The room fell silent, and just in time, the chef was coming up with more treats. Chef Royal came around the corner, asking if we needed anything. We both stared at her and passed her the joint. She grabbed the joint and inhaled for a few seconds. "You guys are dope." She said, and she gave the joint and excused herself. We, on the other hand, were left in a room full of truth, trying to figure out which lie it matched. We kept digging and stumbled across another photo. This time it was dated within the last five years.

It was clear Kyle and Sonjay were involved with my client for a long time. I didn't waste my time showing Tati each photo I found with them, incriminating themselves. I had a bad feeling about this. I am not sure why but the photo I was holding captured a picture of Roe and Jay in a not so good light. I never heard of them having a fling or anything, but I don't understand why they would be kissing and holding hands in this photo. I looked over at Tati, who was digging in her box. I decided to leave this box alone for a moment until I was alone.

This wasn't something that needed to be shared. I had some digging to do, and I couldn't do that with Tati watching. It would damage not only her marriage but the relationship with her sister. I made a note on my pad to follow up with Roe. I packed everything back up in the box and moved it to the side. I took the highlighter and wrote my name on the top of the box. I reached for another box to go through. I asked Tati if she had found anything when we were interrupted by a ringing phone. We both looked around, searching for the ringing phone.

The ringing stopped, and we both stood still. We heard a vibration before the ringing started again. We both held our phones in our hands, and it wasn't ours. We continued to follow the ringing, and it led us to a nook in the back of the bedroom. It was creepy. It had a built-in seat. The phone was sitting out in the open, still ringing and vibrating. I was a bit apprehensive and yet eager to know who was the owner of this mysterious phone. So I grabbed it and hit the answer icon. "Hello?" I said. I turned and looked at Tati, who was begging me to put it on speakerphone, so I obliged.

"Are you the lawyer representing Jessica Fischer?" An unrecognizable voice belched (spoke)? Into the phone. Tati looked at me, shrugging her shoulders. I answered vaguely. "Who am I speaking with?" I asked. Knowing it was rude to answer a question with another question. I had manners, but I was not about to identify myself until I knew who was on the other end. We stood in the center of the nook, waiting on a response when we heard mumbling in the background before getting a response.

"I am calling to see if we could set up a meeting on behalf of a client. I am unable to disclose the client's information until we meet. However, from my understanding, you will be representing Mrs. Fischer. Is that not correct? The lady responded.

I sat for a second deciding what I should say. I let the lady know I work for Ms. Fischer, but I did not confirm being her lawyer. The caller identified herself as the assistant to the lawyer representing a client in the current case in my office. She would like to set up a meeting very soon to discuss the topic at hand. She mentioned allowing things to settle down for a few days before our meeting. I was still confused. I had no idea who the client could be other than Kyle. At this time, there are no additional persons charged.

I made sure to listen because I wanted to make sure I remembered everything she was saying actively. Tati had begun jotting down notes as she continued to talk. I asked to meet with her in the morning because I wanted to talk to her while everything was still fresh on my mind. We talked for a few more minutes when she finally let me off the phone. She ended the conversation, letting me know to keep the cell phone on me at all times throughout the process of this case. I had a bad feeling about her client, but I was in no position to judge. I knew this situation was going to be wrong, but I had this gut-wrenching feeling it would get worse before it gets better. We sat in silence before even giving each other feedback on the freaky call. We both knew we had our hands full. There are areas of town that Tati can go in because no one knows her; I can use that detail to my advantage.

I broke the silence by asking if she was willing to get a little dirty for the rest of the week. Laughter filled the room as we simultaneously realized that we were both in over our heads. I knew we would have to bring in someone else to help us with this case. I grabbed my phone and sent a quick text out to Mrs. Fischer. I also sent one to Roe reluctantly. I had that eerie feeling where I knew I was going to make a lot of new enemies. It was frustrating because it was nothing I could do to make it all disappear. My phone starting ringing, it was Mrs. Fischer. I glanced at the time before answering. It was super late, later than I realized. We were in a zone. I answered before the call went to voice mail.

"Good evening Mrs. Fischer is everything alright?" I asked. She sounded like she had been crying. She wanted to know if I could protect her. She had been getting unknown phone calls, and she felt like someone was following her. I was stunned. I didn't think things would be so dangerous. Who in the heck would want to terrorize her? I immediately placed her on speakerphone. "Are you in danger right now?" I asked, starting to get nervous myself. I looked over at Tati, who had yet again stopped what she was doing. More tears came from the other end of the phone. "Please, just come and get me." She said. I was silent for a moment; I couldn't bring the woman who was accusing my husband of rape to stay with us.

I had to do the right thing. My gut said no, it was getting way too deep. Before I knew it, I was telling her to send me the address, and I will have someone to pick her up soon. We ended the call, and I went to see if I could prepare a ride for my client along with finding linen to set up a room for her. I knew I would be crossing significant lines. I told Tati we would need to find a way to keep the door closed that had all our files. Even though all of this paperwork will help her, I usually don't allow my clients to see me during my research process. I had no time to play; I needed to make sure she was safe. More importantly, who could be after her.?

It took a little over an hour and a half for Mrs. Fischer to get there. I was starting to worry if the location we were in was fit for the circumstances. I spot cleaned the place to make it suitable for my client. I heard the doorbell ring, and Tati's happy ass hops up and runs down the stairs to answer the door. I was nervous as hell. I don't know why by my insides just don't feel right. I feel like we are missing something. It's almost like I am still only getting half of the story. So screw it. Let the little lady in.

We are about to be kind and friendly, and the truth will come out. I hope my marriage can handle this case. The thing was we had an arraignment to prepare for and to be honest, things were still not looking too good for Kyle. I just want to break, but I can't. I stood at the top of the stairs deciding whether or not I should take the elevator. I stood there, frozen. To be honest, Mrs. Fischer was younger, prettier, and built like a brick house. Her weave hung to her bottom, and I was merely jealous. There. I admitted it. Here I am slightly older, no makeup, nor anything fancy to toss on my back to royally stroll down the steps and own the room. Hell, could I blame him for cheating? I can see why. I guess I had become a little less attractive over the years but, rape? That takes things to another level.

I had to snap out of it. They were now both climbing the stairs. Thank goodness they didn't use the elevator; there was no way I could handle them popping up in a matter of seconds.

It took them at least a minute or so to get upstairs. A fake smile was plastered on my face as I kept trying to wake up my brain. People think I am bananas for even doing it, but I am the only one that can handle this case. Before I knew it, my hands extended and embracing Ms. Fischer. Tati grabbed my shirt, letting me know to let go. We went into the library are a few steps down. I felt I was floating. I was in another mind frame, and I had to be honest. I had no idea how to get out. We all grabbed a seat, and the room fell silent. Yet again, Tati came to the rescue and introduced herself. I was finally beginning to snap out my trance when Tati mentioned being married to Sonjay.

Ms. Fischer's eyes got big, and she stood up immediately. "I shouldn't have come here." She said as she began to scurry out the door. "Wait!" I found myself calling out to her. "Wait!" "Please!" I was shouting at this point. She stopped in her tracks and turned to listen to what I had to say. "This is a safe space." I reached my hand out to Tati. She returned by grabbing mine. "This is my best friend. She is willing to be here to help in any way possible. We are both confused as to what is going on, and I need you to help me speak your truth." I didn't take a breath. I needed to make sure I keep myself together. It was hard to keep my composure. I was a ball of mush on the inside. The room fell silent, and Tati extended her hand out to her.

"I won't lie. I want my story out there. This situation is riding on more than just me." Ms. Fischer finally spoke. "I was confused for a moment, but I made a mental note to return to this moment a little later. I shook my head, acknowledging that I was ready. We released hands, and we all sat back down. I took out my note pad that I had been writing questions on and got to work. Tati grabbed her tape recorder. We opened a bottle of liquor that was in the cabinet next to a Victorian bookshelf.

Before I could say anything, Ms. Fischer held her glass in the air. From this point on, just call me Jess." She smiled. It was weird, but we clanked our glasses together.

We poured another shot and got down to the interview process. I explained as much as I knew of by looking at some of the files. She responded by letting me know I was way off and had no clue what happened. After all that schooling I had, yet again I felt defeated. She was about to give me a run for my money. I don't think all the encouraging talks I am giving myself could prepare me for what I was about to hear.

Tati decided to sit on the floor like it was storytime. I turned and looked at the clock. It was super late, and we would be paying for this in a few hours, but I went with it. I decided to pour another shot, and this time Jess pulled out a joint and lit it up. The hatred in the room had come and gone. We sat there playing nice and setting the tone as I prepared to make notes on what Jess had to offer to the case. Tati, on the other hand, was now standing in the corner, staring at the bookcase. We laughed for a few minutes, realizing she was drunk. Poor thing.

As the room settled, I pulled out my joint and told Jess I was ready to hear what she had to say. Jess took a long pull from her joint before speaking. She exhaled deeply, and the smoke made little circles in the air. Hell, she was talented in more ways than one. I had to admit we were all meshing well. I hope we could keep up this energy. Before I knew it, Jess was singing like a mockingbird. She gave us a little history about herself before we got to the meat and potatoes. We learned she was from around the way and got caught up with a friend that did a lot of bad things. Whatever her friend wanted her to do, she would jump on the opportunity because she considered her family.

They had known each other for quite some time. Her friend lived a life of revenge against someone that hurt her and her family. Jess admitted to being witness to a lot of things that she shouldn't have been. She went on to say that when they found her friend's body, she changed her name because she was afraid someone would be out for her next. We were only minutes into this interview, and I needed a big bowl of popcorn and another shot. The things she stated blew my mind.

I had seen a lot of criminals but had only heard about name changes and stuff like that in movies. Tati, as usual, was pouring another shot. She wanted to make sure all stayed awake. I interrupted Jess and asked for that intermission I thought about moments ago. I was buzzed and had to use the ladies' room. I was also hungry again and wanted to hit the kitchen. We all agreed upon a ten-minute break so we could gather ourselves.

I did what I intended to do and took the elevator upstairs. I had a tray full of fruits and veggies we could snack on. It's funny how women can come together if we stop judging one another and hear them out. Some of the things Jess mentioned tonight makes me quiver. She could have been dead right along with her homegirl. I guess I had to admit, though, Jess reminded me of Tati. She knows her husband has something to do with this case, and instead of worrying about her marriage, she is more so here for my moral support. I guess she's down for me like Jess was down for her homegirl. Our time had come to settle in, and things were starting to get serious again.

Jess picked up right where she left off. It was like she was performing a verbal autobiography. Even though the recorder was capturing every word, she spoke. I made a few mental notes on a couple of crucial moments thus far. I realized why God is giving me the strength to go through this case. He needs me to tell her story. I was perfect for this. Emotionally I knew detaching was not something I plan to question. I no longer felt lost and confused as to why I agreed to take this case. It was faith that brought us here together. Jess continued to explain once her friend died, things changed for her. She wanted to take revenge out for who she felt was responsible for her friends' death.

Playing dirty can sometimes come at a cost. She knew a girl that was in deep with her friends' original enemies and got a job working for them. They started her out with clients who barley tipped. She was responsible for being eye candy for the most part. The company sounded horrific. To me, it seemed like modern-day prostitution.

My heart ached for her. She was just a young girl with no real direction or path in life. She must have received excellent reviews from her clients because she received a promotion to be a party girl. They hired party girls to come and perform sexual acts on random people, whether it was male or female. She admitted the lifestyle could get you caught up. For a minute, she had lost her focus.

One night, she met a guy who had followed her around the party all night. He tipped her a thousand dollars just to sit and have a conversation with him. At the time, she didn't know he was in politics. She just knew he would show up to every party she attended. It started with a simple conversation then began to escalate into something a bit more.

I began to pour more liquor into our cups. Tati, baked out her mind, but her face told a different story. She was soaking up everything Jess was saying at this point. She knew the man she was talking about had to be her husband. Her eyes filled with horror. Jess paused for a moment. The room was still, and we were hanging on every word.

I gave her a nod letting her know she was ok to continue. We promised we could handle it. Jess began again. This time confirming Sonjay was the politician, and he wanted to spend time with her more and more outside of the events. She admitted she agreed. He was a good tipper, so she had to jump on the opportunity. One day he asked her to bring a few chicks with him, and she complied.

They kept it going a little over a year. Recently, things began to escalate. I jumped in to ask her what the name of the company was. Jess replied, "El Fetche," I wrote down the name with exclamation marks on the end. We had our first lead. Instead of letting her finish, I wrapped it up for the night. I had what I needed. I knew exactly where to start. We all dispersed and went our separate ways. I went to sleep with one thing on my mind. El Fetche.

Chapter 4: Rico Sanchez (Rico)

Times like this, I realized why I stayed away for so long. I never wanted to hurt Nina, but sometimes you have to get gone to handle some business. X was making things difficult for my empire. I noticed he started moving funny closer to the time Nina graduated school. I knew as a man; I should never put my full trust in another man. I couldn't do anything but blame myself. Hell, if the Feds knew I was still alive, things could go south real quick.

Nina allows me to make it all up to her, but I think she has put me in the friend zone. She acts a little standoffish at times. I guess I get it, though. Who was I to expect her to take me back after everything I had done? I was responsible for the death of Felecia's cook. I sent my goons to take care of her. I wasn't expecting anyone else to be home at that time. It planned out perfectly. A team had followed her into her house. I paid top dollar to put an end to Nina's stress, but the chief walked up on my guy as he was breaking into the door.

Years ago, I would get X to do heavy-duty tasks that require the appropriate disposal. I was highly disappointed a few years back when I found an item he swore he had eliminated. I found that a bit odd, so I started watching him closely. It was all true. When the streets talk, you have to be brave enough to listen to them. X was talking to the feds about my operation. I had to fake my death to see what was going on around me. If anything, it's always the low down women who end up breaking. But my homie? I was not expecting that. I dipped out. I faked my death, and I had to figure out what was happening.

While I was away, I discovered Felecia knew X when she was a kid. He was friends with her daddy before him leaving. Nina didn't remember anything about Felecia. I think she was honest about that. She had been from home to home; she probably had no idea who she was. Over time, I was able to get her to understand Felecia, and explained what part X had in all of the madness.

When things began to heat up between Nina and Felecia, I knew it was time for me to show my face. I couldn't allow them to bully her about tragic events she had forgotten existed. Nina later explained that I caused more problems than what I may have thought. She was so paranoid now. She didn't trust anybody. I couldn't even come over to her new house until recently.

I had to respect it though I was tripping in the past and may have wanted to make things right again I loved her enough then, and I love her enough now to let her do her job without me. I will always have her back, though. She will never want for anything. I think that is why she still keeps me around. Since I am back, she does give me the chance to work at the company. I handle the elite men that need private events scheduled.

I make them pay a very hefty fee for the events, as we generally do not do private outings. Nina said it would be a bad idea from the beginning, but she still was willing to do it since it was my first idea I brought up in a meeting.

No matter what, I tried to convince her I didn't need her to do me any favors, but, yet again, she was right. One of my clients had crossed the line. I don't think the guy ever paid attention to the fact that there were lines. At the time, things were going smoothly. I would get the events in order by coordinating with the client and Tae to see who was available at the time. Tae had a good thing going with her girls, and she brought in millions of dollars to El Fetche. I knew going to her for help would be a good move. Who knew my client was off the deep end? I never met up with the ladies I would simply send them the location. If they did anything hands on that was totally up to them and what they were willing to charge. My nonrefundable 2.5 million dollars per party was enough overhead for them to do whatever they wanted to do. Who was I to judge?

Each time we set up a party, we have a crew film the events. I never go back and watch the film. I felt it wasn't my place to do so. The ladies never complained about anything, so when this most recent event went down, let's just say it was unexpected. We have to roll with the punches and do whatever is best for the business. I say we should simply eliminate the problems from all sides. This matter is going to get pretty ugly. I don't think we will be able to hide the dead body situation. A part of the contract asked all clients never to release information about El Fetche. It was almost like a party at your risk type of situation.

Nina did the right thing by calling us all together to discuss this matter. I take it to the extreme when I make decisions. I am taking the backseat as much as I can. I will try not to interfere. However, if I am honest, I paid a few Cubans to take a visit to Jess Fischer's house. She was coming from the grocery store. I made sure they didn't scare her too much but enough to make her want to drop the case. My intentions were never to run her away. We lost contact with her, and I haven't been able to figure out where she went. Her phone was no longer tracking her location. It was like she disappeared. The Cubans made it clear they did not lay a hand on her.

My thoughts were interrupted when my phone started ringing. I must have thought her up because Nina was calling. I was lying in my bed in the dark. I cleared my throat before I answered. "Hello?" I asked. It was a bit late for her to be calling.

"Hey." She said. She sounded like she was just waking up as well. I remained silent, assuming she would give the reason why she was calling. "Did I wake you?" She asked. I sat up in the bed, adjusting myself to talk to her. "Um, no, I was, I was just laying here," I said. I thought I should have come up with something bright but leave it to me; I had to be honest. "You sure, I just couldn't sleep and, for some reason, wanted to call you." Nina sounded like she was stressed. Usually, when she can't sleep, she stays up all night cleaning.

I guess things had changed since I left. I like this adjustment. She can call me anytime. "You're fine. What's going on?" I asked. It seemed like the moment I heard her angelic voice; I got sleepy. It was almost like my body was starting to relax. She had some kind of power over me. I loved her from the day I laid eyes on her. I was older than she was, of course. I made sure things were legit with her age before me making any move on her. She also had to finish school. There was no way I would date her if she were uneducated. "I just really wanted to hear your voice." She said softly. I knew she must have been in deep thought. This was nothing new. She would call late at night, wanting me to stay on the line until she fell asleep. I simply responded by letting her know I was here to talk whenever she needed

it.

Snoring from Nina filled time for the next few hours. I still couldn't sleep, unfortunately, but I didn't mind. I was actually at peace, listening to her. I made so many decisions that caused her so much pain in the past. I just wanted to be there in any way possible. Things could have been different if I talked to her. Maybe faking my death was the wrong way to scope things out, but I didn't want her to think I was running out on her. That was never the case. I wanted her to understand that if I knew better, then I would have taken a different path.

Moments later, my alarm was buzzing in my ear. Time had gone past so fast. I had to meet with my clients today to let them know what we are facing. Kyle was in jail without representation, so El Fetche has to ensure that he keeps quiet. The tricky thing is the prosecutor of this case, so happens to be Kyle's wife. She was not the type of lawyer that you could pull any backhanded deals around. She was a pit-bull in the courtroom, and she agreed to take this case in hopes of getting down to the truth. She swore there would be no tampering and was required to choose a co-chair. She had not announced the co-chair at this time, but whoever it was, I knew it would only increase the odds of a conviction.

Just the thought of it gave me anxiety, and when it boils down to it, this was my fault yet again. I never imagined things would go this wrong. I decided it was time to wake Nina up. I cleared my throat, which startled her. She began to fumble with the phone. A few moments passed, and she returned to the phone. "Good Morning," she said, trying her best to sound sexy and ended up looking like the wife from Love and Marriage back in the day. I giggled a bit, trying not to judge. "Any morning is good when I wake up to you," I said, trying to be smooth. She laughed loudly for a second. "Boy, please save that Billy Dee crap for them, Cuban girls. You better get up and meet your clients." Nina was fully awake at this point.

I laughed it off and wrapped up the call. Her comment secretly bruised my ego. She makes a way to make it clear she doesn't want me. I had to swallow that with pride because I made this bed. Now, I had to lie in it. It was time for me to bust a move. It was another night of not sleeping, but I knew once I got things in order, I could relax, maybe even ask Nina to take a trip with me. I knew for her to agree I had to take care of this case. I hopped up and began to start my day. I asked Google to turn on my shower, along with some music. I stood in front of my mirror, staring into my own eyes.

I did this every day. I couldn't expect people to see me unless I could see myself. I reassured myself that I was a strong warrior who could not be defeated. I went on to say that today would be a good day. Within the next two hours, I was dressed and headed out the door. I looked good, smelled good, but more importantly, I felt good. Understanding my heritage allows me to speak positivity into my life. I can't front like I didn't learn anything while I was away. I learned how to be a real man. Hopefully, in time Nina could see that, but if not, I loved her enough to walk away. I won't walk away like I did last time. I plan to handle this case and say my good-byes.

I jumped in my truck and headed to the prison to meet with Kyle. He was the first stop of the morning. I sent a text to our lawyer and made sure she was en route. It would only take a few minutes for me to make it there, but I couldn't go in without her. She is listing me as her co-chair at least right now during this visitation. I planned to get him bailed out soon so he could get home. We needed him out to be able to get a good handle on this thing. Before I knew it, I parked in front of the jail. Things were looking up. I could see Rolinda's beautiful self, standing outside on the phone. I knew I had to stay clear of her. She was gorgeous, educated, and feisty, a triple threat.

Since we had our initial meeting, I had to admit she had crossed my mind a few times. Once, she sparked a joint in the board room; to me, that was nothing short of amazing. The whole thing was a slight turn on, but again I have to keep things strictly professional. I love Nina, but a man got needs. I let my thoughts float away in the wind as I grabbed my briefcase out of the backseat and shut my door. I clicked the alarm to lock the door as I walked away. I reached the heavy glass doors where I had to send my items through the metal detector. Rolinda was standing there past the sensors waving her hand. I tilted my head up to acknowledge her.

Once cleared, we greeted each other with a handshake. Rolinda told me to follow her and lead me to the room where Kyle would join us shortly. The room was decent enough for us to conduct business. There were three chairs placed close to a steel table; it was nothing like the movies. There was no big metal gate that divided the space. Four walls and two doors surrounded us; one door was the one we entered in, which lead out to the courthouse and metal detectors. The other door was for the prisoners. We both took a seat at the table, and I pulled out a note pad along with a contract for El Fetche.

Rolinda was the lawyer, and she was also responsible for making sure we all understood our roles in this situation. However, I would be the host of the show when we have these meetings. We opened our files and began to share different approaches. I wanted to hear his version of what has taken place. Within the next few minutes, the guard unlocked the door that was adjacent to us. In walked our client, who looked like someone had given him a pretty good beating. He held his head high as he shuffled through with the chains around his feet. The officer then released him from the handcuffs.

The guard shut the door behind himself, and we began our meeting. Rolinda introduced herself and allowed me to do the same. She pulled out her tape recorder advising it was just to keep a record. "Well, I think we just might want to get down to business," I said, eager to get this done. "Your bond at this time has been increased to a quarter of a million dollars." I paused for a moment allowing things to sink in. Kyle hung his head low. He was feeling it just like I wanted him to. "So, tell me, why are we here?" I asked. Straight to the point with no chasers.

Kyle lifted his head and began to give us his story. "Things were good, man. Everything just got so real so quick." He hung his head low once more. He continued. "I don't know where to start. We had parties every month, and it never escalated to the point where things got so bad." His words were starting to ramble on. Rolinda interjected. "I think we should slow it down a bit. She reached her arm out and grabbed his hand. "We will get through this." She said. I gave her a quick side-eye, but it was clear she needed to save me from tanking this ship. Kyle looked like he calmed down. He took a deep breath, and Rolinda released his hand.

"So, I am going to let you know why I am here," Rolinda said. It seems like she was handling things pretty well. She reached out and grabbed the contract. She presented it to Kyle, letting him know why he had no other choice but to read, sign, and agree. She was handling business. I took notes as they continued to talk. Once Kyle signed the documents, we began to get down to the real market. The tape recorder was still recording, and so far, all we have accomplished was the contracts for EL Fetche. Kyle began to speak, and this time he had a mouthful.

We sat there for another hour—Kyle sang like a canary. I told him that we would get him bailed out in the next 24 hours, and Rolinda put a request to have him sent to the infirmary until he was released. Once we were outside of the prison, we talked for a few more minutes. Rolinda had done a great job today, and she knows what she is doing. As we began to walk towards our vehicles, she hollered out, letting me know to stay in my lane the next time. I couldn't help but laugh. We both were safely in our cars. I watched her drive away while I sat there, sending a text to the other client. I needed him to know I was on the way.

Sonjay was a little different. It was clear from Kyle's story Sonjay was the aggressor. This hit hard a little bit more than Kyle since Sonjay was already a client of ours. As I let my car cool off, I waited on a response back from Sonjay. It didn't take long. He responded, sending me the address where we could meet. Surprisingly I knew exactly where this location was. It was rather close to El Fetche Headquarters. I didn't mind this location at all. Once I wrap things up with him, I could stop by the office and ask Nina for a lunch date. I'm sure there will be plenty of things we can discuss. It was going to take me a little over thirty minutes to get to him.

I hope I can handle things as smoothly as Rolinda. I should have made her come with me to this meeting as well. I had intended things to go differently than what they did. I figured I wouldn't need her for the second meeting. I secretly regret making that decision. I did at least take a few notes from the meeting with Kyle. I am hoping it will allow me to make a sound but strong impression. Before I knew it, I was pulling up to Sonjay's office. It was his campaign space. He had a pretty sweet setup. A man like him stayed caught up in something scandalous. I don't understand what would make men in power jeopardize everything.

One day, women will get to the point where they realize they have power between those legs. I have seen all kinds of men from different walks of life, and they all fall. Moments later, I was face to face with a murderer. I couldn't hold it against him too bad; I had done my thing a time or two. The difference here was, the people I have harmed were never anyone good. I don't know the young lady, but a man should never do females like that. I tried to gather myself as I greeted him. I smiled and wore my game face, and I was assuming he was doing the same.

"Glad you could sit down with me, Sonjay. I know you're a busy man." I said in a snarky tone. He returned the same energy, letting me know it was his pleasure to sit down with me. We chuckled a bit, and right on queue, I pulled out my briefcase. His face changed as he realizes just as Kyle did. This case is a big deal. His eyes met mine. I immediately let him know I would hope next time we meet in better circumstances. Sonjay shook his head in agreeance. "I met with Kyle earlier. He gave me his outlook on things, and I want to extend the same courtesy." I paused and continued.

We have already taken a big leap by including your "homie" in on your services. We need to make it clear that at no point will you associate this incident with El Fetche'." I met his gaze once more as he was now moving around in his seat. I took it upon myself to go to the deep end. I was honestly disgusted with him. The images from our conference were replaying in the back of my head. I could see the girl lying there, helpless. "So, tell me something, why did you do it?" I asked, still not breaking my gaze. Sonjay was very uncomfortable. He kept looking around and adjusting the buttons on his jacket.

"Look, man, I don't know what you're talking about." He said, slightly smiling, like everything he did was ok. Before I could even think of a response, I was yanking him up in the air with the table still between us. Once I realized everyone had now begun to pay attention to the commotion, I slowly placed him back on his two feet as his smile jumped from his face. He knew it would be a difficult task to prove he murdered the girl, but it's cool. I made a mental note to make sure everyone knew he was a killer. He had no remorse.

I had nothing else to say. While he stood there straightening his clothes, I grabbed my belongings and turned to exit the building. Sonjay stood there, clapping his hands, chanting for his crew to get back to work. Before leaving, I turned and gave him a good look down. He had my skin boiling in anger. I couldn't believe at no point did this man show any remorse for his actions. How was he planning to lead a city in the right direction? He was crooked. I would make sure El Fetche's name remained clean throughout this entire situation. I think we should hang him out there to dry.

I got in the car, slammed the door, and beat my fist on the steering wheel. I wanted Sonjay to feel me so bad. He needed to show some respect. I turned the AC on and allowed the car along with myself to cool down. I had to adjust my thinking to get through this. I connected my phone to the car and sent Nina a text. I needed to just be in her space. My head was super cloudy. I want to do the right thing by protecting what Nina has built. I started thinking of a plan on how I was going to bring Sonjay down. He was not going to get away with this.

"Hello?" Nina answered the phone, sounding frustrated. I guess my energy had rubbed off on her before I even called. "Hey lady, you good?" I asked, not wanting to transfer my bad vibes. "Nothing just a long day, what's going on?" She asked. I could tell she was trying to adjust her tone a little, and honestly, I appreciated her effort. "I just wanted to take you out for lunch if you can get away from work," I said, holding my breath, hoping she would say yes. I was still sitting in the parking lot while Nina debated on letting me take her to lunch.

"Sure, I can escape, plus, there is something I need to talk to you about." She was almost back to herself at this point; I didn't know if she had something good or bad to tell me, but that didn't matter. I shook off my thoughts and pulled out my parking space. I was only a few buildings down from her. I let her know she needed to start locking up for lunch.

We ended our call, and minutes later, I was parked in the parking deck waiting on her to come out. I had no idea where I would take her for lunch, but I was sure anywhere she wanted to go, I would take her. Cali was known for good food and a good time at any time of the day. I waited an entire thirty minutes before I saw her walking towards me. She was beyond beautiful. She was wearing a strapless black dress with a red lace sheer cover over it. I had to catch the drool from falling down my chin. She opened the car door showing me all her teeth.

"Thank you for waiting for sir." She said as she closed the door. "Did I have a choice?" I asked playfully. "So, where you taking me?" She asked. I kept it real and shrugged my shoulders. "As long I am with you, it doesn't matter to me," I told her, knowing she hated when people asked her to do something, and there was no thought put behind it. I'm the opposite. I'd instead make it up as I go. Things are more exciting that way. Well, in my opinion. Surprisingly she didn't get frustrated. She had taken it upon herself to put enter a new destination in the navigation. I had no idea what she had up her sleeve, but I was following her lead.

We shared small talk as Nina caressed my neck. Her touch was so soft. It was like I melted every time she was around. I was no good. The sun was out all day, but dark clouds now covered it. Today had to get better. The navigation chimed, alerting us that we had reached our destination. The building was lighting up the entire block. The valet opened my door as we parked. I looked over at Nina, who was already waiting for me at the base of the massive stairwell. She never ceases to amaze me. I grabbed a few things out of the car and allowed the valet to drive away. I met Nina at the staircase, and I held out my hand to accompany her.

Before moving, I leaned over and kissed her on the cheek. She giggled, and we walked up the steps. We bypassed the front counter, filled with desk clerks assisting people dressed in the most elegant attire. I felt underdressed, and I was wearing a suit. I was slightly embarrassed for being unprepared. Nina must have recognized me overthinking and squeezed my hand. I snapped out of my thoughts and allowed her to continue to lead the way. We ended up in front of a golden elevator. Surprisingly she didn't push the up arrow; instead, there was a green down arrow that glowed as we waited. My mind was yet again puzzled. I held back once more, trying to think if I was packing any heat. Nina didn't allow me to carry anything when I was with her, but I was feeling insecure.

The elevator arrived, and the people aboard made their exit. We stepped in, and as soon as the doors closed, Nina pushed me against the glass, palming my manhood. My temperature was rising, but we arrived at our floor. I thought this was a hotel; instead, we were in an upscale underground casino as long as you gamble drinks and food items are free. We quickly found a table where we're able to view the menu. I was stunned. She would always turn me on to something new. She pulled out a cigar from her purse and lit it.

I can't lie; at this moment, I was blushing. Looking around, you could see the elite of the community; money was everywhere. I needed to compose my inner thoughts, but my eyes were everywhere. I couldn't focus on just one thing. Nina could tell my anxiety was taking over, so she made sure to give the waiter our food and drink orders. She squeezed my leg, calming me to the point where I could relax my other leg from shaking. It took a few minutes, but we were finally starting to unwind and enjoy ourselves. It didn't take long before the half-naked lady was bringing us a tray of shots. I didn't remember ordering this, so I tried to stop the waitress.

She turned and said it was from the couple in the back. Nina and I both looked around for familiar faces, and there were none anywhere in sight. We went back to our world. Our real drinks had arrived, and we clanked our glasses to an adventurous lunch. It didn't take long before we had a table full of empty glasses.

Before we knew it, we had spent two hours eating and drinking away. Nina asked if I had something to get back to for the evening. I couldn't think of anything else I'd rather be doing than her. We stumbled our way back to the elevator, this time we went upwards to the top.

It took us at least two full minutes to get there. We made our way off the elevator and into the penthouse suite. Nina must have had this planned all along. I thought it was sexy; she took charge. I never plan anything like this. We opened the door to the penthouse, and the couple from the bar was in the living room waiting for us. Surprisingly the attire they were wearing earlier in the evening had suddenly vanished. I turned to Nina, making sure it was ok to enter the room. She giggled and told me to let things flow. She didn't have to tell me twice.

I immediately began to undress, pulling Nina entirely into the room. We exchanged passionate kisses as we stumbled over an accent chair. We both stopped and laughed; it felt like the old days. Nina pushed me down on the bed, but I realized as I floated through the air on the way down, a sparkle caught my eye. I turned to see what it was. It happened to be the couple from downstairs. How in the heck did they get up here, and why were they here? I was wearing confusion on my face. Nina kissed my neck and whispered in my ear. "Remember, just let things flow, enjoy yourself," she said. I didn't want to, but I promised I would. I closed my eyes and allowed things to play out.

Two hours later- Nina and I were cleaning up in the shower. We were inseparable. She got on her knees and took my manhood inside her mouth. I let out a loud gasp. This stuff is what I missed, the spontaneity of us. I didn't want to force things, and I had to admit letting things flow felt pretty good. We both reached our happy ending several times.

I was exhausted, to be honest, but I knew I still had more work to do. Now was not the best time to talk to her about the meetings I had earlier. I didn't want to put a damper on things. We cleaned up a bit before we left; we were those kinds of people. We never want anyone to know what has taken place behind the closed door. We would even pull the sheets back. Judge me all you want, but I have no idea the name booked under this room. Reputation is key. I left a hundred-dollar tip on the nightstand.

We left this beautiful piece of heaven behind as we drove away. We decided to call it an early business meeting, I dropped her back off at the office and I headed home. Today was so long but far from over. I turned up my music and rocked out. My phone was going off again, and I clicked my steering wheel to answer. "Talk to me." I was surprised that even came out of my mouth. I was clearly in a good mood, thanks to Nina and her associates. "Aye, I can't find her still."

I heard one of my Cuban goons say. I snapped out of that happy place and got down to business. "You still can't put eyes on her?" I asked. My tone was now changing. I couldn't believe they couldn't find this girl. "We will keep looking, and we should have her by sundown." He said, trying to reassure me that things were going to be ok. I didn't respond. I simply disconnected the call.

It didn't take long for me to get home. I honestly didn't feel like getting out of the car. I wanted to figure out where

Miss. Fischer could be. I decided to have Rolinda give her lawyer a call and see what she could find out. I sent a voice text to Rolinda. She responded before I could press the button to turn off my ignition. She confirmed she would reach out, but I didn't respond. My phone vibrated again as I shut the door, this time it was Rolinda. She asked if we could meet up later tonight. I hesitated before responding. I will wait until I get inside to return a response. I wanted to think about this decision before I did anything I would regret later.

Like a typical man, I got into my house as quickly as I could. I tossed my bag down on the counter. I immediately began to pull my phone back out. I hadn't thought of anything to say but instead of giving a direct answer. I asked what she wanted with me at this time of night. She giggled through her text and responded, "It's just business." When it came across my phone, I shook my head. Nope! I said out loud. I am not falling for this. I didn't respond. Instead, I placed her contact on do not disturb. I will remove it in the morning. Tonight, I needed to show restraint. I wanted nothing more but to mount on top of her, but I can't risk losing Nina. Especially after the day I had with her.

I continued to unwind by taking a hot shower. I was on the prowl for Mrs. Fischer. It was clear I couldn't trust my Cubans to get the job done. My mind was racing, and I kept seeing flashbacks of this afternoon. Before I knew it, I was stroking my manhood. It was something about Nina's eyes that drove me crazy. I have no idea the kind voodoo she has on me, but I can't shake her. I could hear her moaning in my ear as I tried to finish washing. Within minutes of my flashbacks, I was reaching my climax. I knew I had done way too much because my knees were shaking. I was struggling. I let out a burst of laughter, and it echoed throughout the bathroom.

This girl had me straight tripping. I needed to remember who I was. I used to be the king of these streets, but I had to make different moves. I had been apprehensive about stepping back into the game. I have to admit I miss the power. I wanted to make sure I stayed under the radar when I came back. I didn't know how I would regain my control, but once this case is over, we shall see how much things change.

I stood in the mirror, wiping off the steam. I stood there. I was just analyzing things. I knew tonight I had to search for Mrs. Fischer. I'd instead meet with her rather than her lawyer. I wanted to see if there was anything we could offer her. She was considered one of our employees, but we decided to stand with the client as he had the most significant risk with the dead body situation. Tae made preparations to make sure Mrs. Fischer had everything she needed to retire early from El Fetche'.

She had brought us plenty of money, but we would expect her to be a bit more careful. When things began to turn south, it is a procedure to contact security immediately, and they will get them safe. The problem with that we had only approved a certain number of private events. Our security team still covered each event. Going outside of those parameters can cause issues such as the one Mrs. Fischer is now involved in at the moment.

It didn't take long for me to get dressed. I pulled up my tablet and started doing additional research on Mrs. Fischer. She was tough to find at first, but I was able to hack into her mainframe on her computer. She had a shallow security setting; it was like she was begging for someone to hack her. I was able to see she had reached out to her lawyer. I guess the Cubans were right. They had scared her into hiding. I didn't want things to go down like that, but I would be the one to fix it. She had her phone linked to her computer, which was perfect. There was a text that was deleted from her phone but not her cloud. I took a screenshot of the address.

I continued looking into some of her documents. Maybe, I had all I needed to do what I needed to do to silence her. There were photos and home-made porn videos. She had plenty of people on film. Almost all her clients were on here. That is totally against the rules. What was she doing with this stuff? I continued searching for ammunition I could use. I stumbled upon something a little too personal to be in her documentation. There was a photo of Nina on one of the folders on the desktop. I decided to copy everything at this point. Once I clicked the photo of Nina, several subfolders popped up with more pictures of people who were a part of El Fetche'. My interest was at its all-time high; I had to resist temptation and stop digging.

I quickly went through my nightstand drawer and found my flash drive. I decided I needed to see all of this on my monitors. I scooped my cell phone, tablet, keys, and anything else I needed before I left the crib. I turned on my hot spot and made another copy of her entire modem. Anytime she uses her computer or phone, I will know. I grabbed my backpack and stuffed everything in sight. The tablet was still downloading on the flash drive. I clicked on my alarm and headed out to my lab. My lab is at El Fetche's headquarters. Nina had finished my space on the very top of the building. She consumed the majority of the floors with the new expansion. However, my area was secluded.

No one even knows there is a floor besides the architect, Nina, and me. I quickly hopped in the truck and made my way back to the office. I had a feeling I was on to something. If I could get all of this data analyzed, then maybe we can figure out what in the hell is going on. I had no problem with letting Nina in on this information, but I needed to comb through it first. I can't let her see her file. Emotions will start to be a concern once you see something personal. Calling Nina was going to be on the to-do list, but I think she would rather see this all in order first. I did, however, reach out to my Cubans headed to the address I found earlier. They had strict directions to sit on the location. I didn't want to disturb anything just yet. I wanted to see what was going on first.

I had a private entrance to get into the building. It may sound a little extra but, me being back may not be a good thing for some people. I had a few enemies before disappearing. We built an underground entrance that required its own parking space; I was on some real Batman type stuff. It was cool. I finally parked and grabbed my book bag and began the quick walk to the elevator. I continued to check behind myself to make sure no one had followed me. Once I was sure the coast was clear, I hit my keys, which luckily simultaneously opens the elevator doors. No one can enter without it. Nina holds the other key. She was determined to get two keys just in case of emergencies. I chuckled, thinking about the things she does to prove she is in control. I turned and pressed the only button available.

It was a quick and easy way to the top. Once the elevator stopped, I stepped out, greeted by "homeboy," it was a virtual assistant. I called him George. It was a built-in system that allowed me to connect automatically via Bluetooth. I always felt like I was home. Nina decked out my entire space in all black everything. She had me digging the vibes in this space, and I was more of the laid-back type; I didn't need much to be happy. As I walked through the office, the lights came on one by one. Things are much more comfortable when it's just me, myself, and I. I asked George to brew a cup of coffee and turn on Bob Marley. I sat down at my desk, admiring the city. It was beautiful at night, and everything lit up as usual. I started to unpack my bookbag. Once done, I walked over to the kitchen to grab something to eat.

Nina makes sure I have everything I need, even when I am out of the office. She goes to the grocery store and replaces anything that is missing. I grabbed a cookie from the pantry and decided to get started on figuring out what Mrs. Fischer is doing. I sat down and began to get settled for the night. My tunes were on; I was secure in my space. I sat down and started digging. It didn't take long for me to realize I was not finding out what I wanted. Mrs. Fischer may not be who she said she is. It seems she may know Nina and an old enemy Felecia.

I had three monitors displaying pictures, and two showed documents where she changed her name. Felecia's estate was hers. It was no reason for her to be working with us at all. According to her bank records that I pulled up on my primary monitor, she should not be worried about money. Felecia had a lot of assets.

Buckhead county records showed land and several house deeds; this is mind-blowing. I decided to print out everything. I had to dig a bit deeper into the motive here. Times were hard trying to put things back together after all the damage Felecia caused. Hell, we are just getting to the point where life feels good. I can't have Nina reverting to being paranoid, looking over her shoulder, and afraid to leave the house.

I will make sure to protect her at any cost. I grabbed my phone and checked in with the crew. They were still sitting in front of the house; one team parked in the front and the other in the back. I asked them to stay put. I decided to hit up an old friend to see what he could do to help. I felt like I was brushing off dust from an old wood box.

George, please dial Brandon. "Dialing Brandon." The system repeated, and it began to ring. I continued to search for more on this hard drive. Mrs. Fischer was thorough, and I had to give her credit. After two rings, the line picked up. "Yurp?" A tired voice answered. "Long time boss," I said. Brandon cleared his throat. "Aye, what's going on, man?" he asked. He sounded more like himself.

"I was hoping you could help me out on a project." I cut straight to the point. I needed someone that I know would get the job done. Brandon had his ways, but he was on point. It didn't take long for him to agree. Within seconds I was getting a text from a burner phone. I quickly responded with the address. He would be the only outsider that knows of this location. It was bright things were way more profound than we intended. We had to do what we had to do. We said our goodbyes. I decided to lay down while I wait for Brandon. If I didn't know anything else, I knew I needed my rest. It was GO time.

Chapter 5 –Tae

It had been months since this whole situation started. Things were beyond messy. Business was good as usual but mentally I was a wreck. I couldn't understand why we were always stuck in something. Life was good. We picked up the pieces after Felecia tried to destroy us, I didn't think we could recover; but we did. I am getting older and quite frankly I was getting tired of it all. It was time to retire soon. I could feel it in my bones. I want to make sure I leave out on a good note. I can't retire and leave my girl hanging. I have been doing more office work rather than attending the events.

We will remain successful, but somehow, we always get a reality check. It lets us know that we are still killing the game and important enough for people to waste their energy on us. We welcome the challenge, but it isn't easy. Times like this I was glad to be well endowed. I needed to take a vacation, but I knew it wasn't the right time. Things had fell silent after we had our initial meeting. There have been a few whispers around the office about a few things, but nothing has been said publicly about the case.

So far, El Fetche's name has not been in the media. I can't say the same for the other parties involved. The trial date has not been set quite yet but I volunteered to be in the court room every day of the week. What people don't know is me and Jess have been cool, I wouldn't say we were the best of friends, but my heart goes out to her for having to deal with being abused. The problem is, I am starting to think there is more to the story.

I wanted to meet up with her, but she had been ignoring my calls. Something must have changed her mind because she text me asking if we could have lunch. I declined and advised I'd rather her meet me at the office.

She hesitated but she agreed. She did however ask that we meet prior to or after business hours. I agreed. It was time for me to start my day. I sat for a few more minutes giving myself positive affirmations. I had already showered but needed to leave the house. It was my safe zone. It was time to take on another challenge. I felt like the repair man for these ladies, I use to be ok with it and now things are unbearable.

I got up and slid into my shoes. My purse was on the counter, I grabbed the phone and left. I wanted to make it a very productive day, so I ordered a few dozen doughnuts on my way into the office. The great thing was I didn't have to stop and get out the car to get them. You place in the address of your transaction and a cute delivery boy with the tight shorts delivers your order. It takes little to no time getting to work. I recently moved closer to the building. Nina had a nice spot on the outskirts. I wanted to be closer to the office.

We had hired Jodi full time and it took a while for us to trust her. She earned some cool points over time. You know how it is? People can do things to you, work their butts off to prove they are different. Yet, we as unforgiving flesh tend to save face by forgiving them in the moment and secretly writing them off. Jodi is still a part of the company. She is just at arm's reach. The doughnuts were right on time. I could see the steam rising from the box.

They were fresh. I hadn't made it to the office, but I could see the delivery person on the security camera. I was just pulling up, so it was perfect timing. I would tip a few dollars more for the wait. I wasn't one of those lazy people who got everything delivered. I thought about the economy. We all must make a living. It was another way of feeding my community.

I pressed the greenlight button on my phone allowing the delivery person to step into the forum area of the building. I wasn't worried about him doing anything as

I prepared myself to get out the car. Security was already up and ready for the day to start. I scanned into the building and greeted everyone. "Good morning!" I said and everyone returned the same energy. I signed for the doughnuts and provided the nice lady with a hearty tip. She thanked me and wished me a great day.

I turned and let security know I was expecting a guest through the employee entrance. I continued to my office and my phone started to vibrate. I looked down and it was Mrs. Fischer. I stepped into my office and quickly got settled. "Good morning. This is Tae." I answered knowing I really didn't feel like having this meeting. "Hey its Jess." I looked at the phone, thinking to myself obviously. I had to of course remain professional.

"Yes, I am here at the office. I am ready when you are." I said. Letting her know she better not have me out of my bed for no reason. "Perfect. I will be in shortly. Is anyone else there?" She asked and I ignored the question. "I will be waiting for you." I said and quickly ended the call. I allowed my office door to remain open. The glass had slid into the perfect spot. Just enough to say, come in but yet enough to say stay out. I sat down and began to bring up my system. I generally like to take my time and clean out the email box.

I browsed through upcoming events and responded to a few clients who wanted to book a date. It didn't matter what time of day it was; my plate could sometimes be loaded. Hopefully, Mrs. Fischer is coming to tell me she is dropping charges. It didn't take long before I began to hear a faint knock on the glass door. I picked my head up and smiled. I stood up to greet her and I returned to my seat.

We said our pleasantries and I pulled up her employee file. I asked why we were here. She hung her head low. For her to be so ashamed she was dressed to the tee. It was still cool in the mornings, yet sister was sporting a short leotard. Her hair was snatched from the Gods. Who knew we would ever get to this point? I remember when she first came here. I was tossing her some nice gigs. Whatever she was doing worked. She told me once that for a while she would never agree to sleep with any of her dates. She said she kept it super professional. I was dying to know what changed.

She took a deep breath and started talking. "Have you ever thought things happen for a reason?" She asked. I was one of those people who had to be delivered from wearing my thoughts on my face. Jess picked up on my opposition. "Well, I guess so. Depending on the situation." I answered. I was intrigued on where this was going. Prior to allowing her to come in, I brought up a recorder. I wanted proof of this conversation. Honestly, she could be doing the same thing.

"There is a lot that you do not know about me. Prior to me coming here I was a totally different person. I first want to say thank you for this opportunity to work here." Jess begin to relax in her chair. Her demeanor was speaking to me. I couldn't figure out what it was saying exactly but she has my attention. I pushed back in my seat, to give the impression my guard was down. I crossed my legs and cleared my throat. "I can honestly say that you were a good boss."

She said. I was starting to understand what was going on. "Ahhh, I see. This is your resignation I assume?" I asked. I knew at this point I had to be careful with my words. I continued. "It has totally been my pleasure to be your boss." I said staring her down. She was still unbothered. "I wouldn't say I was resigning; I have simply decided to become an entrepreneur; you can say." Her tone had now turned petty. She was playing games and I was not here for it. I asked is this what she needed to come and tell me.

She said she had more in store. She then turned angry admitting she was pissed we as a company did not stand behind her in this situation. She wanted to know what El Fetche was going to do to accommodate her. The room fell silent. I had to process. I needed to process. How did I not see how slick this hoe could be? Slowly but surely it was all making sense. It is about money.

I shut my eyes before responding. There was no way I could give her an answer. I had to contain myself. I was not going to be the person who was caught on tape admitting or negotiating. "Ms. Fischer. Coming on board with us has totally been a great relationship. I totally understand not wanting to continue the relationship. Prior to accepting this position, we offered a contract. We will continue to honor said contract as we hope you will. I do want to be clear when I say this.

During your employment here we have a strict policy on private events due to something like the current unfortunate events. I believe you may want to speak with our counsel if you are wanting to renegotiate your contractual agreement." It took everything out of me not to revert to my old ways. The old me, would have got straight to the point. The professional me, always has to ensure I secure my bag.

I am not sure what kind of reaction she was expecting to get out of me. I was not interested in whatever she was trying to get down with. I quickly asked was there anything else I could help with. She caught my drift quickly. I am sure my face confirmed what I was feeling. I had already uncrossed my legs. I stood tall with a smile. I adjusted my clothing and walked over to the glass door. I pressed the button on the wall and the glass slid over. I held my hand out facing towards the door.

"It was totally a pleasure meeting with you today." I reached in my pocket with my left hand and pulled out a business card for Rolinda. The urban in me showed up for a few moments. I turned my head to the side letting her know I was tired of standing there. She stood up. Walked slow. I mean abnormally slow. It was like she was either trying to come up with a comeback or she just wanted to pick her face up from the floor. Either way, today was a waste of space time and energy. My thoughts are simple. Get out. Before she was fully out of the office, she thanked me for having her and promised we would do this again real soon. I didn't respond.

I simply pressed the button to close the door in hopes of catching her heel. She was so lucky. I walked back over to my computer and ended the recording. I immediately got on the phone with Rolinda. I needed to let her know I was sending her a file. I let her know it was a little over an hour. She didn't sound too excited, but I had to send it to her. I couldn't believe this girl had the audacity to think we would give her hush money. She would lose that case.

However, exposing what really can happen here could be the issue. I decided to stay in the office today and comb through her file. I wanted to take another look at her contact and check the dates we booked her for. I wanted to make sure there was nothing that could possibly jeopardize El Fetche'. I had to dig deep. Things just don't add up. I was pissed on the low. I had plans for the day. I did not intend on things going so left. May the cookie crumble where it may.

I just wanted to make sure I was doing the right thing. Nina sent me a text a few hours later letting me know she was on the way in and had started to round up the staff. She wanted to see if we had any updates. I grinded my teeth together. I continued to dig up things on Jess. Surprisingly, there was literally no record of her. I mean, I found simple things like her current address and phone number.

There was nothing that showed high school records or college degrees. I printed out everything so I could bring it to the table. Something was fishy. I have no idea what, but it was not my job to figure it out. I will let Rolinda see everything and whatever she decides will be best. I refuse to get sucked back into this place. I love the work I do but the stress is on a whole different level. Time was flying past and I hadn't noticed.

My secretary sent a message asking should she tell the others to go on without me. I didn't realize it had gotten so late. I told her to give me a few moments and to order lunch for us all. It took me a few minutes to compose myself. I headed down the hallway to the board room. Before I placed my hand on the scanner, I took a deep breath. I knew it was game time. The glass door slid back and allowed me access into the room. All heads turned making my tardiness even more awkward. "My apologies team. I had my head stuck in some work." It will not happen again."

I said apologetically. I bypassed a few people and sat down. Nina smiled as I took my seat. I am sure she is judging me, but it will not last for long once she sees what I was working on. Everything had begun to settle down now that I had arrived. All the chatter stopped. All of our attention went to the packets that laid before us. The monitors that were built into the table began to display our logo. Moments later Nina advise us we had another presentation and she would be sitting down but still presenting.

That was weird, she loved having meetings. She says it is her time to mingle with her folk. The lights dimmed and things become serious. The volume was turned all the way up. It was video footage that was leaked to the press. It showed two men carrying a limp body out of the room where Mrs. Fischer said her attack took place. Police are now looking for someone to identify the body that was found. What could we say? We have not been identified yet so we should be in the clear. Well, for the moment at least. We continued watching and I decided to whip out my note pad and take a few notes. I wanted to compare what Jess said versus what is being reported on the news. It was disheartening that we are watching her lifeless body float through the hotel hallways. What pisses me off the most is when we asked if there was any footage the owner swore; he didn't have anything. At this point, my eyes were glued to my monitor.

Outside of the two men carrying the body, we saw another clip showing Jess at the hotel days prior. She was booked in the same exact room. I paused my monitor and began to comb through some of the files I printed earlier. I guess I was making a lot of noise. Everyone's attention was now on myself. I stopped shuffling papers and looked over and asked what I had done. They all laughed and pointed out the fact that I controlled the other monitors. I didn't know that at all. I paused theirs causing them to give me their undivided attention. Nina cleared her throat through her laughter.

"Since we are all listening can you share with us what you're looking for?" She asked now starting to walk over to my side of the table. I couldn't help but to laugh and shake my head. Technology was never my thing. Nina sat down in the chair next to me. She was still laughing. We were a whole mess in that office. I think it was good to get a little laughter in the room. I explained I was looking for dates that I had printed out. Just as Nina was reaching her hand over to help me, I had found what I was looking for. According to our records Jess had no reason to be at the hotel.

To be honest none of the locations I had listed for her dates were on that side of town. Nina grabbed the other papers I had shuffled through. She quickly read over the documents I had realizing that there is something more to the story. She also told me I had done a great job of bookkeeping and would like to get some help on her files. She started passing out everything I had printed. I had to admit having my files displayed across the table made me feel crazy. I knew deep down it was for the greater good. I allowed it. I did however; press play to take their attention off of my documents.

My plan worked until there was something else that caught the eye of another El Fetche member. They joined Jess at the hotel days prior to the incident. Quickly the main monitor changed and the gentleman at the end of the table began scanning the face he collected from the footage.

We all shifted our attention to the front. The T.V. chimed. It found the face from the hotel video. It was Jodi. Our security manager. She was also involved with the fiasco with Felecia. The hair on the back of my neck started to stand. It was almost like I could feel the drama that will soon erupt. I stood up and addressed the team. "I have a hunch. I am usually a better judge of character.
I dropped the ball. THINK! If Jodi is popping up in some shady stuff, I am sure it is in revenge of her homie Felecia." I looked around the room to see if anyone was feeling what I had to say. Nina's face showed she was processing what I was saying. Rolinda finally chimed in. "I have been provided with several new pieces of tid bits I would like to add." I was hoping someone else would chime in and she did. Right on time. She continued.

"Something is totally up. I am having a tough time figuring it all out. I guess now is the best time as any." Rolinda was acting weird. She went on to say Jess Fischer is not who we think she is. In fact, Rico came across a lot of evidence showing Jess was actually Jasmyn. How in the world did we not catch on to this? Everyone in the room was wondering who Jasmyn was.
Things where literally buried. There was no need to let people know about the situation when it had already been handled. It was one of those need to know type of situations. Nina interjected. "Rolinda, I think this is a conversation that we should have in private. We want to

ensure we are releasing facts. Sounds like we need to double check a few things." Nina said as she quickly brushed passed us all and grabbed Rolinda and they both exited the room. We all sat there for a few minutes. Once I noticed they were not coming back I took charged and pressed play on our monitors once more. I already knew

Nina would fill me in, so I wasn't too worried about rushing off to catch the tea. The video started once more, now that we all knew who was identified in the video, we had more understanding. There were several clips of Jodi and Jess coming in and out of the hotel over the course of a month's time. We were all shocked. The film showed them coming and going freely sometimes with bags and sometimes without. Who knows what they were carrying in there? This is yet again, another reason why I didn't like the idea of hiring Jodi in the first place.

Nina wanted to give her a try preaching everyone deserves a second chance. The clips had finally come to an end and there was nothing else we needed to discuss. I asked the team to list any questions they have about the film and send a group email. I allowed the team to leave. I stayed back and cleaned up the office. We were a messy group. Trash and papers were everywhere. I couldn't just leave it all behind. I gathered all the papers that were on the desk and did my best to get it together.

Nina left so fast; they didn't grab all of the documents Rolinda brought to the table. I put down everything I was holding and started looking through some of the papers. It was clear Rolinda was telling the truth. It was clear what I found earlier was spot on. I was looking at her Jasmyn original birth certificate, a copy of her id, and a copy of all her documents under Jess Fischer. What I don't understand is what is her end game? That mess with Felicia is over with. We thought Jodi had turned a new leaf. She had come a long way. She never missed a day. She has hired an amazing staff of security members. I continued to clean up as much as I could. I walked out the door and headed back towards my office. I wanted to pack up for the day. I honestly wanted to throw this whole day away. As I am approaching my desk, I see a group of people walking towards one of our private rooms. We only use those rooms when there's a big wig the office.

I knew I hadn't scheduled any appointments today. Nina hadn't mentioned anything to me about a meeting. I was debating on whether I would interject myself into the room or dismiss myself for the rest of the afternoon. Despite my desperation to get out of the office, I couldn't fight the urge. I rushed down the hallway meeting Nina at the door at the same time. We both looked at each other and she asked what I was doing here. I looked at her and told her because I am nosey. "Hurry up girl, we gone be late."

Nina said as she smiled and rolled her eyes as we pushed through the private volt. All eyes turned to acknowledge the late comers; I bowed my head to give my apologies. We found an open sofa to sit on. Everyone had their serious face on. I was starting to think I should have carried my ass home. I took my time scoping out the room, just to see who all was in attendance.

Surprisingly, Rolinda was here sitting in the corner at a round table with two chairs. She was accompanied by another female. I couldn't make her face out. It was too dim. I didn't want to assume it was her dirty client, so I didn't bother speaking. Nina sat beside Rico. There were two other men in the corner of the room standing by the built-in bar. This room was for the exclusive clients. We had everything we needed.

There were a few monitors that I could access in case of a security breach. Nina cleared her throat and got things started. She had her business face on, she asked everyone to get closer but not too close where they are uncomfortable. I looked around to see who would move. I stood and walked over to the corner next to Rolinda.

Rolinda and her plus one walked over towards Nina and Rico. We all shifted. I wanted to be secluded. I shouldn't be in here anyway. There was no need for me to have any input. I was obviously here as a spectator. The rule had always been to leave our phones in the safe. This kept a certain level of discretion. I had broken that rule. I immediately decided to stick my hand in my bag and sit down where Rolinda once was. The bartender quickly wiped the table and allowed me to order a drink. I kicked back and watched the show.

The meeting had begun and Rolinda still hadn't introduced her guest; who was still holding her head down. Rico had the floor and was introducing his clients. Both Kyle and Sonjay had graced us with their presence. I was shocked to see them both here. As Rico stood tall and began to talk about his clients. He mentioned we needed to ensure all parties understood why they were here. We were all ready to get this over with, me more than others. Nonetheless I made sure the recording button was on because I had no intentions on missing any of this good tea. Rico mentioned things would be challenging since Sonjay is denying any involvement with the incident. Kyle on the other hand sat with his head down, his wife was staring a whole in his head. Rico continued to advise that Sonjay is here in full support of Kyle.

He wanted to let Kyle know he would make sure any fees would be taken care of. Kyle stood up abruptly and made it clear that he was guilty of having sex but not guilty of a murder. Everyone in the room froze. It was only a select few that knew about a murder. Me personally, I was taken aback that he blurted it out so candidly. Tyesha reacted before we knew it. She was now in her husband's face. She was pissed as she should be. Rolinda wanted to reel Tyesha back in. She needed to remain professional but that was out of the window. This was clearly the first time she was getting a chance to hear her husband speak the truth. She wanted to talk to him more but now was not the time. Her client began to squirm at this point, she was totally uncomfortable. It is going to take a lot more manpower to keep Tyesha away from her husband.

She was hurt and had every right to be. The woman he is admitting he slept with is her client. She should have recused herself from this case. I can see why they make people do that who may be close to the two parties. Nina finally jumped in the mix and shook a bell bringing everyone to a halt. The room fell silent and we all turned our attention to Nina and Rico who were now standing in the middle of the dissipating couple. It was intense, I sipped on my little cocktail.

I disappeared into the shadows and took notes on everything. I was waiting on the perfect time to interject. I was completely positive Jess was actually Jasmyn. I stared at her even more now. It was nothing I could do to really prove it physically. I know Nina would get some better details on this situation, but it wasn't the right time. The waitress came to offer more drinks. Before she could deliver the ones that were already ordered Tyesha's hand knocked the tray from her hand and in reaction Nina pushed Tyesha to get it together. I was frozen.

Things were getting bad. Instead of recording audio only I decided to film this fiasco. Who knew all of this anger would pop off? Nina called my name asking me to help with mediation exercises to calm everyone down. I chuckled thinking to myself these people need more than meditation and breathing exercises.

They needed prayer. I gulped down my drink and held my cup in the air, motioning the bartender to whip up another. I straightened my clothes and stepped out of the darkness. We were in the situation room. It was no need for emotions to get the best of us. "Well, now that we all have had our five minutes, do we want to talk and come to an agreement or do we want to take it to trial?" I asked. I still hadn't removed my eyes from Mrs. Jess Fischer. I was pissed about this situation on the low. "I would like to ask you all to remain standing.

It's clear you're light on your toes. Any objections?" Everyone looked around, even Nina didn't speak up. I continued. "Kyle, you are one of the problems, just not the main problem." Sonjay cleared his throat. Tyesha directed her attention towards Sonjay. "I think you have something to say right?" I asked. I crossed my arms and even faced him. The room was calm. I had no idea things would get under control so quick. I think everyone is actually looking at the enemy.

I still had my eyes on Jess. She was also looking at Sonjay. She held her head down once she glanced up briefly making eye contact with me. I stepped closer to her and she immediately shifted. It was clear I was better at this mediation then the people who get paid the big bucks. The difference here is I had nothing to lose. We all stood there in silence. I cleared my throat letting Sonjay know I was waiting on him. He looked over at me and stood up. "I didn't come here to get blamed or shamed into admitting something I didn't do. This is a rape case. I hadn't heard anything about a murder." Kyle looked at Jess and back to Sonjay.

They obviously don't know about the video we were able to find. My drink had arrived, and I asked the staff to pour a round of shots for everyone in the room. Tyesha asked Sonjay what his involvement in this matter was. Just as he was preparing to give a mouth full of lies the shots were being passed around. I went to the bar and quickly grabbed the remote attached to the countertop. I joined the group and took the last shot from the staff. I stood in the middle of the room. I don't know if it was the two drinks, I had prior to the toast but I was overly confident right now. "Everyone let's lift our glasses. To finding out the truth." All of the glasses clinked together in agreeance. I pressed play on the retractable monitor. I dimmed the lights. I asked them to remain standing until the film was over. I went back to my corner. As the video played the faces in the room began to shift. I felt like a naughty witch, who just ruined the party. Everyone who had not seen the video was horrified. I actually loved watching Sonjay.

He was pissed and looking for ways to stop the video. I could see his hands trying to move up the wall to find a switch. I laughed for a moment before walking over to the bar and pouring myself another shot. I whispered to the waitress and advised her to bring a round of cocktails. We were getting to the best part. The room was filled with music in the background from the night in question. Kyle began whispering to Rico.

Oh, the room was uncomfortable. I was loving it. It was something about having the sense of control and watching everyone crumble around you. God don't like ugly and I think we are all tired of dancing around the issue at hand. I honestly think there is more to this story but only time will tell. The liquid courage I keep serving is bound to bring out some truth. The music in the background went off.

I pressed pause to give someone the opportunity to speak their mind. I walked closer to the group who were all looking at me. "Round table time people." I said as I laughed and took a seat. I extended my arms out letting them know they could sit. Everyone slowly sat down, and the waitress delivered the fresh drinks.
The waitress winked at me as she walked back to the bar. In each drink, I have asked that she add an extra shot for good luck. I plan on tipping the staff pretty well to ensure their secrecy on the matter at hand. I sat back in my chair and crossed my legs. Nina began speaking to Jess.

"Mrs. Fischer, why exactly are you persisting we have a full trial?" Nina wanted to know what she really wanted. I think I was pretty interested to that as well. Tyesha interjected. "I think I would like to know why my husband is on the tape having sex, not raping you." Jess took her cocktail straight to the head and held her hand up for another. Jess was now in the hot seat. Funny how a little video footage can change the perception of things. These were pretty good questions. We all sipped and awaited to hear her response. I had some questions of my own but that can be addressed later.

"Listen, I think it is imperative we go to trial because people need to know what has happened to me. Reality is, yes, I had sex with your husband on several occasions. This video is a joke and a wacky attempt to scare me off. I won't have it. You should all be ashamed." Jess said. I placed my drink on the table and slowly clapped my hands. This girl is a hoot. "Now that she got the best performance of the year award can we get some realness in this room please?" I asked. It was clear I was feeling my drinks, but I was on a roll. Why stop now? Nina agreed we all needed to be more transparent and remove our emotions and egos. Rico chimed in as well. Tyesha didn't break her stare.

We knew if she could talk right now and remain professional with her paying client she would. I was still in disbelief about why she would even accept the case. It wasn't my man, so it is not my business. Kyle stood and approached his wife. She held out her hand stopping him in his tracks. She was pissed all the while she never blinked. Jess pushed her lips in the air and continued talking. I was silently praying she would just put us out of our miseries. "I slept with Kyle, as I stated before but that still won't change the fact, he was forceful with me the last time. Yes, we all watched him kill my homegirl." Before she could continue Sonjay jumped from his seat and was now choking Jess. He was screaming at her to shut her mouth. Rico and Kyle pulled him off her. Sonjay was furious. He kept yelling at Jess.

"You low bottom piece of nothing. I should have killed you. I knew you was a liability." He was spitting with each word he spoke. My phone was still in the corner getting all of this on film. Tyesha tuned to Jess and asked once more. "What is it that you want from this?" Jess smiled and said money is nothing if you don't have power with it. I know I will be paid for a lifetime to shut my mouth but on the other hand why not shoot for the stars. I want El Fetche. I worked my ass off to be an entrepreneur and now we are all here.

This is my time." She sat back and chugged her drink. She knew she was holding the cards. She was right about one thing; money was nothing without power. Nina was in the corner laughing so hard. I couldn't quite catch the joke. I was amused by simply watching this play out. Things where getting out of control once again. I took out the controller and pressed play. Everyone stopped in their tracks and the room settled down once more. I didn't waste my energy this time by standing.

However, it was clear the group couldn't handle it. I paused the tape once more. "I am going to ask that you all stand back up. I think things are more productive that way. "They all did as I asked. Once they were standing, I asked that they bring their concerns to the forefront once more. No one said anything. I pressed play. I had nothing but time. I was going to keep playing their game until they were tired of playing it.

The room was now filled with the sound of Kyle telling Jess how good she feels. You could hear a slapping noise in the back. Kyle must've had a little freaky side in him. Tyesha was mortified. I knew it had to hurt her to go through this. I was two sheets in the wind to even care.

Things were starting to escalate between Kyle and Jess. They changed positions.

The camera was a perfect shot to Sonjay. I paused the video. I didn't want to do this. I wasn't a heartless monster. I don't want to continue to torture the room with these small clips of porn that was essentially evidence. Sonjay was still standing by the door. Rico was approaching the group. The screen was in a frozen frame of Sonjay and the girl we all now know he murdered. Tonight, can change a lot of moving parts to this game. Things will not be the same for sure.

Nina walked over to Sonjay asking him to join us so we could get this over with. Of course, there was another round of shots being brought to the forefront. Sonjay finally came to join the rest of us. Nina suggested I press play again. Before I could Sonjay was finally ready to talk. "So, things may have gotten a little carried away, If we could simply settle this issue and move on; it would be great." He said as he took his hands out of his pockets. I understand he wants to bury this issue, but he would need to take responsibility for it and suffer all of the consequences.

Jess on the other hand wasn't amused. She looked pissed. Her plan to take down El Fetche was starting to crumble. I was still trying to figure out what gives Jess the idea she could take over. I just needed to be a witness to every attempt. Somethings you just have to see for yourself. I know she was Felecia people. The issue is bigger than El Fetche, the issue was me. I hired Felecia not knowing she had a major vendetta against Nina. She talked me into hiring Jodi. You're never supposed to buckle under pressure.

I should have stuck to my guns. The sight of Jess and the courage of these drinks almost made me lose my religion. I have had enough. I stood and walked over to the bar. This time I went behind the bar and grabbed a bottle of Vodka. My anxiety was climbing to an all-time high. I knew my time in this hell hole was coming to an end. We were literally going nowhere. I took the bottle to the head for at least ten Mississippi's. I gathered myself and shook off the bickering.

My ears were even tired of this madness. I whistled loudly bringing the talkative group bringing them to another halt. "That is, it!" I shouted. "I have had…" I stumbled a bit and Nina interjected. "Sis maybe you have had enough." Nina said. Causing everyone to laugh. I am glad they are choosing to find so much light in this dim room but yeah, I was at my limit, In more ways than one. I could give that to her. I was willing to own my faults. I joined in on the laughter for a moment then my face turned stone cold.

"But I mean what I am saying. I really need us to handle this like educated adults. Jess, should I call you that or Jasmyn?" I asked? My words where slurred. Everyone began looking around confused like I was crazy. Jess on the other hand looked like she had been compromised. I wanted to take things a step further. I kicked off my heels and walked over to the intercom by the door. I pressed the green button. I may have held it a bit longer than usual, but the wall felt good when I applied my body weight against it. I released the call button and a familiar voice responded. "Security. Everyone ok in there?"

The female voice asked. "Yes, everything is going swell. Could you get someone else to cover the front desk for a few minutes? I need your help in here." I responded. I stood by the door until I heard the door unlock. My zebra print elephant was seconds away from walking into the room. Once the door slid open, she walked in and the door immediately latched. She looked around and I ran my fingers across her shoulders.

"Thank you for joining us this evening." I said as I lured her into the room towards the group by her black clip on tie. She was a bit apprehensive but once we stepped into the light my immediate focus was Jess. She was frozen. She didn't move. I adjusted the lights a tad so everyone could meet my little friend. "Everyone. This is Jodi. Some of you may know her as the security guard at the front desk. However, there is way more to this beautiful woman than what meets the eye."

I gave Jodi a moment to speak to everyone. She didn't say anything. She simply nodded. "I bet you all are wondering why she is here. I was hoping our friend Jess could shed some light." Jodi spoke up before I could continue. "I am not sure how I can help you. Is there something I need to do?" She asked confused. Jess still didn't have the balls to step up. Tyesha turned to Jess with the same face as Nina.

"We don't have all night" I said. I was a bit aggressive at this point. Jess sucked her teeth before she spilled the beans. She talked for what felt like forever. Everyone sat down one by one like the domino effect. Nina listened with intensity. I could see the fury in her eyes. I was starting to second guess my decision on bringing Jodi in here. Maybe now was not the time. Nina stood and interrupted Jess in the middle of her confessions. "Ok! I have heard enough. Jess, this case is over and if you want to walk out of here without a hair harmed on your head you will agree.

Rico, you need to decide what kind of businessman you want to be. Kyle, I see no issues with you other than cheating on your wife repeatedly. Sonjay...." Nina paused for a moment. "You will pay Jess a settlement amount to keep her silence.

You will then also dissolve any associations with El Fetche. In addition to paying El Fetche' two point four million dollars within the next seven days. Failure to do so will result in the releasing on this tape. Jodi. I would hope you understand how much I wanted to see you win.

Unfortunately, your time here is over." I think that was the most difficult part of the evening. Nina wanted to have faith for Jodi. She knew what she was dealing with being caught up with the wrong people. She always had a thing for "fixing" people no matter how many times I would try to convince her not too. I felt bad in this moment. I should have handled this a lot differently. I can't front it has been fun to watch it all unravel.

Nina asked if anyone had any objections. Jodi tried to plead her case that she left her in the past and that Jess swore she was coming to work here with good intentions. She claims she didn't know it was her at first. I personally was tired of hearing her talk while playing on Nina's heart strings. Rico must have been feeling the same way I was. He kindly asked for her keys and identification card. He opened the door and walked her out. Since there were no objections in the room Nina left shortly after Rico. Jess gathered her belongings and asked if she could leave. I was the only employee left in the room outside of the bar staff. I held my hand in the air motioning for one of the two to come to me.

I asked for them to walk her to the door and ensure the overnight security guards went to do a clean sweep. It was code word for cleaning our files and adding new encryption since we just let go of Jodi. Before Jess left the room, she stooped down in front of my chair. She pretended to drop a napkin on the floor.

"You're a mess." She said in a snarky tone. She rolled her eyes as she was walked out the door. I could care less about her thoughts. I came, I saw, and I conquered. Even though Nina was the one who actually thought of the final arrangements to this disaster. I felt I played a part in getting to a very doable solution. We plan to keep things under wraps, but we also get paid. We will not bury this incident. Sonjay is on his own. El Fetche is in the clear. Yet I didn't feel good about things. Jess can't give up this easy.

The only person she could go after is Sonjay but there was something about some of the things she said that keep repeating over and over. I noticed Kyle and Tyesha lagged behind. He was begging her to forgive him. She kept trying to walk away but he would pull her back. I didn't want things to escalate. I interjected myself into their moment. "Hey guys it's getting late. You ready?" I asked. I did my best to remain calm and speak clearly. I'd seen so many small arguments that turn deadly real quick. Tyesha looked relieved at my interrupting them.

"Yes, I am. Can we go?" She asked. In my world that meant, thanks sis. I got up and held my hand out. She latched onto my hand and we began to exit the room. Kyle grabbed the bottle I had sitting on the table. He hit me in the back of the head. "Don't take her away from me." He said as I fell to the ground. I hit the floor so hard. I didn't have anything on me or around me that I could use to fight back. I tried to crawl and grab his leg. I couldn't see what was going on.

My head was hurting so bad. It felt like I was sweating. I could hear muffled sounds that sounded like screaming. It was a lot of commotion. I couldn't breathe. It was strange, my heart was racing, and I couldn't catch my breath. Things around me became more distorted. I felt like I was fading away. At times, I could hear movement all around me. I was in and out, but people were surrounding me. Their words sounded muffled. I couldn't make out if it was a male or females voice. It sounded like I was under water. My ears felt like they were throbbing. I coached myself as much as I could to get up.

"Come on Tae. You can do this. Get up." I repeated it over and over. I could feel my fingers and arms starting to move. My limbs were so heavy. I don't know if my attempt to save myself was successful. I tried to roll but I felt like I was under a set of restraints. My eyes were felt like I was looking through broken glass. So many lights were flashing. It went dark that moment; well it was longer than a moment. My thoughts stop. I couldn't tell if I was sleeping or dead. I wasn't in any pain.

Which was weird. I knew I had fallen but forgotten how I fell. I gave up. I stopped trying. I was tired. I just wanted to blink really hard. My eyes had to be closed but I still needed to feel something move. It was like I was trapped inside my own body. A steady beeping noise continued to tickle my ears. I was hoping I was in the hospital, but it had a familiar sound of a car alarm. I was so confused. Since I couldn't move, I tried to yell for help. My throat felt like I had something in it.

My mouth is so dry. I couldn't be in a hospital; they would have given me ice to stay hydrated. I don't feel anything running through my veins. The voices started to fade. The beeping was now a long chime. I was cold. I had goosebumps on my legs. I realized maybe things were really bad. If this is the end of my life, I realized I may not have been a good person. I'm going out alone.

At least I feel alone. Ever been trapped in your own flesh. Almost like the dreams you have that wake you up in the middle of the night, but you can't wake up. A ton of bricks sit on your chest and the only way out is to pray. Mama used to say if that happens you living wrong. I guess she was right.

Chapter 6- Tyesha

"Kyle what did you do? I screamed at the top of my lungs. I pushed him out of the way, it was bad enough he smashed a bottle on the back of her head, he was on top of her ramming her head into the floor. Me and the bartender were trying to peel him off of her. I begged him to stop but he just kept ignoring me. I decided to throw myself on top of her. I took a few blows from him until he realized it was me. Blood was everywhere.

Tae's body was limp. Her breathing was so shallow. If it wasn't for her subtle moans, I would think she was dead. I laid on top of her to shield her. I couldn't believe my husband was this monster. It was like he is a totally different person. "Somebody help us please!" I screamed. "Please!" I pleaded. Kyle stood up and backed up from Tae's body. I was so scared. He was standing there with his hands on his head. It was settling in. He began to pace around the room the bartender left us. We were locked in here with no way out.

The monitor on the screen showed Kyle getting oral from my client. I don't know what I was thinking. I should have denied the case. Tonight, was a lot to take in, but Nina came up with the perfect solution that made everything right in the world with the case. My relationship on the other hand was over. There was nothing else I could say about it. If I had any hope of us mending this relationship, his brutal attack on Tae was vicious and I was beyond hurt; I was afraid of him. I didn't want to move from covering her. My birthstone necklace was dangling in her face, so I knew I had to get off her.

I peeled myself off her slowly, I was drenched with her blood. My back was killing me where Kyle punched me. All of our cell phones had been taken once we entered the room. I had no idea where the box could be. Kyle was in the bar drowning his sorrows with a bottle of Hennessey. I was disgusted and I must have been wearing that emotion on my face. He slammed the bottle down on the bar causing the tip jar to fall over onto the floor. I held my hands out in front of me trying to calm him. I used a very low tone and began walking slowly towards the bar. "Ok, let's calm down. We need to think right now."

I said as I took a step towards the bar. "Don't be patronizing counselor." He said forcefully. "I am far from an idiot and I don't need you or anybody else to tell me to think." He begins to walk from behind the bar. He was smiling devilishly. "Ok, your right. I'm sorry. We have to pull it together Kyle. Right now, so we can get out of here." I pleaded with him, this time I took a few steps backwards. He was getting closer to me. He was still wearing a sinister smile on his face. I was freaking out. Tears began to drip slowly from my eyes. Was he going to hurt me like he did Tae? "See women like you, work my last nerve.

You think you know everything. I'm here to tell you the real deal. He said as he began to unbuckle his pants. My eyes were focused on his hands. "I'm here to tell you I am the Alpha. See I let you think you hold all the power. Nah, baby. It's me." He continued. At this point he had me backed into a corner. He was so close to me I could tell everything he had to eat today in addition to his many drinks. I stood on the wall with my hands in the air. I didn't want to make any false moves. I didn't want him to think I was about to attack him.

"You like it when a strong black man takes charge? I hate to tell you Ty-eshaaaa!! You want me to treat you like these rats in the street?" He asked. I was scared to answer so I considered it a rhetorical question. His wet lips began to swallow my face forcefully. I felt so violated. I hadn't noticed he successfully completed unzipping his pants. I began to beg him not to hurt me. He laughed and grabbed my hair and drug me to the bar. I hit my head on the chandelier? in the bar causing the lighting in the room to spin. I felt like I was in an alley being assaulted by a junkie. Instead, I'm here with the man I vowed to love forever. He bent me over the bar and clinched my hair tighter. I was screaming to the top of my lungs for him not to hurt me.

He ignored me. This enraged me even more I tried wiggling my way out of his grasp, but he overpowered me. He ripped off my underwear and inserted his manhood with thrust?. I screamed until I lost my voice. It hurt so bad. He was pounding me so hard I was leaving fingernail marks in the bar counter. My fingertips began to bleed. It felt like an eternity. My body was limp. I had no more energy to fight him off with. I felt dirty.

He released himself inside me. The moment he let go of my hair I dropped to my knees in pain and sorrow. What just happened? Did he just rape me? I thought Sonjay was the sexist. Turns out It's both of them. I was trapped with no way out until my eye caught a glimpse of a red dot that sat in the corner of the room on the table. It wasn't very bright in the room. Other than the dim lighting from the bar and grey screen from the monitor I could barley see the furniture in the room. Kyle stumbled over to one of the chairs we once gathered.

He took off his shirt and wiped his face. He had a mixture of sweat, blood and hate all over him. I waited a few minutes until I knew it was safe. I was going to take my chances and crawl across the room until I could see where the red light was coming from. It wasn't long before I heard my husband snoring.

I guess when you full of that much evil you need to take a power nap. I shook my head in pure disappointment. I legit married a monster. I would have never known in a million years he would subject me to so much disrespect. It was time to make my move. I slowly, moved along the wall until I was close enough to see the light. It was a cell phone. I couldn't believe someone was recording us this entire time. I quickly grabbed the phone hitting my toe on the stool. It made Kyle shift, his breathing and snoring slowed down.

I held my breath and did my best to stay in the shadow of the room. I pressed end on the recording and began to dial 911. I was trembling and my back was in so much pain. Every time I breathed in my side felt like a knife was in it. I dropped to my knees once I heard the operator answer. I was going to be saved. I began sobbing not realizing the snoring stopped. I tried to gather myself to respond back. "911 Operator."

A male answered "Hello, I need an ambulance. I am trapped in a private room." I began to whale. I just wanted to go home. I wanted it all to be over. "Please calm down, can you tell me where you are?" He responded "I I .. I am at El Fetche' Head quarters." I said as loudly as I possibly could. "Your phone is breaking up ma'am, do you know your attacker(she didn't say anything about being attacked)?" He asked. I tried to crawl to another spot in the room. Before I could even move Kyle grabbed one of my legs causing me to drop the phone.

The phone slid across the floor. I began to scream, but trying to remember what I could do to keep Kyle away from the phone. I used what I had, my voice. I had to use a tone from down in my soul. My voice had been going in and out. I started to kick Kyle off me. "TYESHA MCNEIL, KYLE MCNEIL- MARRIED COUPLE, HUSBAND CHEA…."

I felt something break against my back. Blood began to come from my mouth. I started coughing. He begin to kick me in my stomach. I was trying to get away from him. I continued to shout out random details in between my coughs. If I was going to die, it would not be in vein. He was going to go down. "RAPE, ABUSE!" I shouted. He kicked me once more, this time it was on my arm. I heard a loud crack. I was in so much pain. I couldn't move. He saw I was down. He walked over to the phone and pressed end on the call. That was my only chance. I couldn't lift my head to see what he was doing but I could feel the vibration of him walking he must have been going back to the bar to finish what he started. I could hear the steps getting closer.

I heard his zipper go down just as I had before. This time instead of molesting me, I felt something wet trickle down my face. He was taking a piss in my hair. I closed my eyes and started praying. After he relieved himself he walked away. I could hear clinking of glasses or bottles. He must have been pouring himself another drink. The sound of pouring continued which was unusual. Then another clinking of glasses. I realized he wasn't pouring himself a another drink, he was pouring multiple bottles of liquor out. I thought he was simply pouring it down the drain until I felt the wetness drench my entire body, he filled something and dumped it all on me. The room returned to silent as if he had taken a break from torturing us.

I heard the clinking once more. He was filling up once more. This time I wasn't touched I can only assume he splashed it on Tae. He began his sinister laugh he displayed earlier. "I thought you were my forever. The moment we face a little adversity you want to give up on a nigga. They say behind every strong black man is a strong woman right? Tuh" He laughed once more. "I should have known you could never play the part

. I ignored it though. I thought you were different than the other girls." I didn't respond. I continued to let him vent. I wanted him to talk if he could in hopes of the police showing up. Listening to him saying girls in a sense of multiple ladies. How long has he been cheating on me? Why does it even matter right now? My mind was blown. "You remember in school how we would see things on the campus news about missing students?" He asked. "I guess you can say me and a few others had a hand in all of the mayhem." I tried to talk but nothing but a bloody cough happened. "You say something baby?" He asked. I rolled over on my good side and sat my back up against the broken barstool. He broke the entire chair on my back. He was ruthless and I never knew it. He would show up at my dorm late nights.

Sometimes he would have scratches on him but would tell me he gets carried away with scratching his eczema. Its obvious I believed the hype. I was the typical dummy from the beginning. My thoughts began to drown out everything he was saying. I deserved to go out like this I had been the biggest fool of them all. I wanted to just die. I don't know how many women my husband has hurt. My thoughts were interrupted when I saw a spark in the corner of my eye. I used the wall to stand up.

I tried to walk but couldn't move as quickly as I thought I could. I did my best to keep close to the walls. Kyle had his back turned and was sitting at the bar. I moved really slow, my adrenaline was pumping. I was in survival mode. Tae was still unconscious. I couldn't help her. I wanted to. I was unsure if she was still alive. I saw a statue sitting on one the tables under the monitor. I peeked to see if Kyle was still posted up at the bar. He was covered by a huge cloud of smoke. I was content with continuing to grab the statue. It felt like something I could accomplish without being seen. I got back on my knees and crawled to my destination.

I could hear Kyle mumbling to himself. I quickly grabbed the statue and headed towards the door. We couldn't get out the room until Tae let us out or someone opened it from the outside. We were trapped and it was clear the police were not coming. As soon as I reached Tae, Kyle turned slightly in his chair? causing me to stop moving. I didn't want to alarm him. I didn't hear anything else so I continued. Tae was laying in a pool of blood. Her hand wouldn't reach the access point even if I hung it up. I sat next to her body feeling defeated. He won. I couldn't believe I was in this predicament. I stared a hole in the back of his head. I was filled with hatred. I wanted to take the statue and bash his head in. I noticed the cloud of smoke that originally covered him was now a faint trail of smoke. He was dosing off with the cigar in his hands. "Hey Kyle!" I shouted trying to get his attention. I noticed Tae's finger jumped.

She had to be still alive. I tried to squeeze her hand. Her skin was so cold. She must be losing too much blood. My heart broke for her. I tried to shout his name once more but he didn't respond. Before I knew it, his flame had began to ignite the liquor that was spilled on the bar. The entire room lit up. The flames were starting to heat the room. The glass on the bar began to break from the heat. The flames hadn't come to our side of the room yet. I quickly tried to stand once more. There was a closet next to the door. I'm sure someone has left something to cover me and Tae. The fire demolished the monitor.

We were next. I couldn't get into the closet. It was locked. I hopped back over to Tae and noticed Kyles entire top torso was on fire. He was still sleeping through it. He was in a liquor coma. I began to cry realizing this was it. I stooped down to Tae. I began coughing due to the smoke that filled the room.

I laid on my stomach and placed my face on ground. I covered my nose and mouth with my hands I figured it would muffle the smoke. I prayed and thanked God for my family. I also asked for forgiveness for sleeping with the devil. I said amen and my body began to heat up. My blood felt like it was boiling.

I screamed as my body cooked in this dungeon. This was it..... may God have mercy on my soul. I prayed through the pain as my fleshed bubbled. Lord, please help me to remember the power of forgiveness, and please help me to extend this to [insert name(s)]. I know what it means to forgive, and I know all the things you have forgiven me for. Almighty God, our heavenly Father:

We have sinned against you, through our own fault, in thought, and word, and deed, and in what we have left undone. For the sake of your Son our Lord Jesus Christ, forgive us all our offenses; and grant that we may serve you in newness of life, to the glory of your Name. Amen.

Chapter- 7- Jodi

I bet Felecia laughing hard in her grave right now. I played the field on both sides and now look at me. You would have thought I stole from the company by the way they snatched everything away from me. I need Nina to know I wasn't jeopardizing her company. Jess needed a job and she was acting like her head was in the right place. I still loved her. I wanted to see her win just as I use to think she wanted the same for me. Felecia was toxic. I was glad she was out of the picture. I made good money with Nina and the crew. I was literally tossed out in front of the building in a white tee and my boxers. They at least let me have my wallet and cell phone back. My keys were even laying on the ground by the sewer. I held my head down in pity. I liked my job.

I was all in the client's business. They were freaky. It was fun meeting new people and seeing my people make legit bread. I was getting paid here. I grabbed my items from the ground. It was going to be the last time I took a stroll to my assigned parking spot. I hit the unlock button and opened the door. I reluctantly pressed the button to start my ignition. I didn't notice someone was sitting in my back seat. It was Rico.

I didn't realize he was there until the parking garage light reflected against his gun. He was smooth. I had no idea. I chuckled a bit. "Come on Rico." I said as I continued driving. "What's this all about?" I asked. I didn't want to show him I was nervous but I was shook on the inside. I reached the street to exit the garage. "Turn right." He said. His baritone voice was serious. "Last year you and your girlfriends caught Nina slipping.

This year we not playing them games." He was cold. I did as I was told. I was driving slow, way below the speed limit. I wanted to prolong the inevitable. I think he noticed what I was doing. He pushed his pistol against the side of my neck. "Drive bruh." He said. I floored it. It was a natural reaction. It caused him to jerk backwards dropping his gun. I pulled the parkin break up causing the car to stop immediately. Rico fell forward this time hitting his head against the head rest. I hopped out the car still half naked from being violated at El Fetche.

I opened the back door and grabbed the gun. We were sitting in the middle of the road and I was now in control. Rico was trying to compose himself. I think he got the wind knocked out of him. "Get out. Get out the car." I demanded. He looked at me as if I was some little girl playing with a toy gun. I bucked at him attempting to show my power. He complied surprisingly. I wasn't built for this. I just wanted to go home.

Today was unexpected. I walked to meet him in the back of my car. I was still holding the gun. I stopped walking but he continued to come towards me. He stopped just as the gun touched his abdomen. He was taller than I was. Instead of being afraid he was challenging me. He took his hand and embraced mine while he slid the gun up to his chest. "Where I'm from when you hold a gun to a man, you plan to use it. What's the plan shorty? Someone is bound to call the police. How many cars have passed now while you standing here playing?" He asked. His tone was still cold.

He was right though, we were sitting ducks. I turned and saw multiple cars starting to slow down. I was bringing a lot of attention. "Walk away." I said as I began to walk backwards to my door. I hopped in the car and locked the doors I released the emergency break and pushed the gas. I left Rico standing there. In the middle of traffic. He was still in the road. Unbothered. I could hear people beeping their horns to get out the way. I continued straight until he disappeared out of the review mirror.

That was a close call. My Bluetooth screen began to light up. Someone was calling in. I was still shaken up and hadn't decided where I was going quite yet. I ignored the call. I decided to go to the ATM and withdraw as much as it would allow me to. I couldn't go home because my actual address is on my employee file. When they actually brought me on I was temporary.

Once I proved my loyalty I was brought into the security lab where my fingerprints and current housing information was required. There was nowhere I could hide using the same fingerprints. I just hope they don't have connections outside of this poisoned city. It was time for a change but I didn't know it was going to be the kind of change that resulted in me fleeing. My screen began to light up again. This time I answered. I also pulled a joint out of the glove compartment.

"Yeah." I answered. I wanted to make sure whoever it was knew I was not in the mood. "Oh my God. Jodi. You're alive!" I was taken aback. "Um, yeah. I'm good who this." I asked trying to figure out who else knew Rico was trying to kill me. "Jess. I mean Jaz." She said in a very soft tone. "Nah, he didn't kill me. I'm still breathing luckily." I said. I was surprised she called me. I am no good to her now. "Wait! Who tried to kill you?" She asked. Which made me realize she was talking about something completely different.

"Nah, what you was calling for?" I asked. No need to bring her into my mess. "Shortly after I left I heard the fire department racing down the street. El Fetche' is all over the news. It is on fire.!" She shouted with excitement. "Felecia is watching out man." She laughed awkwardly. I was uncomfortable with this conversation and instantly thought of the ones left behind. "Did everyone make it out?" I asked.

"When I left everyone was still in the room including you. What did you do?" I asked. I was legit concerned. We all grown and its time to let all this petty mess go. My heart was racing harder than it was with Rico in the car. The thought of Nina being hurt shattered my heart. I wasn't in love or nothing but maybe I had a distant crush. She was beautiful, smart but most of all a hustler. I felt like my heart was in my stomach. It was a pit of pain. "I don't know. I don't care.

If I get what was promised. Also, no I didn't have anything to do with it. You're welcome by the way, since I called to make sure you were still breathing." She was angry. Before I could respond the screen went black. She disconnected the line. I couldn't focus on her at this time. I needed to make sure everyone was safe. I saw a bank I could use to get cash but I didn't want to stop.

I wanted to turn around and check on Nina. She worked so hard to get to where she is. I made a mental note to check on Jaz later. It was better for me talk to her when she calm anyway. Sometimes silence is the best response. My mind was everywhere. Was Rico cleaning house? I need to know if Nina is ok. I wasn't settled. I wanted to simply leave and never turn back but the thought of not knowing if she was ok was sickening.

Everything else that was on my to do list had to be placed on hold. I continued to search for a good spot to pull over so I can look into things when I realized Rico wouldn't be at my house waiting to kill me. If he was Nina's right hand he should be wherever she is making sure things are ok. I couldn't take it anymore. I was burning up from the inside out. It didn't take long for me to make it home.

Before I parked I rode around the neighborhood to make sure no one was watching me. I didn't see any unknown vehicles for the most part. I was scared to be honest. I looked around before exiting the car. It looked like the coast was clear, it was time for me run in the house. I didn't want to die. Especially since I didn't have time to explain myself. I wanted to clear things up. How could I if Nina was inside the building.

My soul wouldn't let me sit down, I ran into the house as quick as I could. I had to enter my alarm code. So far I was feeling secure. I made sure to place the alarm back on so I could walk freely around the house for a moment. I wanted to shower at least before leaving back out. I needed to take full advantage of being safe in this moment. I quickly grabbed my suitcase set from the front room closet and rolled it to the back of my condo. I had upgraded from the projects.

A lot can change in blink of an eye. I had to admit. Once I proved my loyalty with Nina she made sure I had a place to eat at the table. She gave me another chance at life just if I did my job. I tried not to do things that could jeopardize my stability. Not only did I want to make sure Nina was ok, I just needed her to also know I wasn't trying to cross her. I walked through the house turning on lights to make sure I was still alone in the house before I showered. I didn't want to get out the shower. It felt so good to wash off the drama from the night. I needed to get a move on things and pack a bag.

I didn't know how long I would be gone but I know I needed to ensure I had enough clothes to last. When you on the run you don't have time to stop and buy clothes by the day. I guess you could do that when you're a billionaire. I wasn't built like that yet and Jaz has damaged my opportunity to reach that goal in life. I turned off the shower and grabbed a towel from the wall. It felt good to be home. I don't want to go anywhere. This was the safest place I could think of.

Maybe I will be ok if the alarm is on all the time. I wanted to convince myself it was a fool proof plan but just thinking of last year I have seen what they are capable of. I saw my phone lighting up, last time I answered it was bad news. I was a little apprehensive, so I let it ring. I thought about it once the screen went black. That was exactly what happened when I was in the car. I ignored that feeling and turned on the tv that hung above one of my dressers. I wanted to see what was on the news about the fire. I continued packing just in case I felt the urge to flee. I wanted to be prepared.

My place was nice but I didn't hold any additional security other than my alarm. I was never the one who was "about that life" even though last year felt like it. I was in the middle of my thoughts when the news began to have a breaking story. The music news played suspenseful right before the head chair tells us there is a breaking story after the commercial break. I folded a few towels and watched commercials of political campaign ads. I wasn't interested in anything political. I escorted many of them through the back entrance of El Fetche.

They were all snakes if you asked me. No ones asking so I keep things to myself. The music came back on for the breaking news. I stopped what I was doing and sat at the edge of the bed. I grabbed the remote and turned up the volume. "Tonight on GFH News, we are reporting a breaking story coming from downtown. We will reach out to Gregory who will give us the latest update Gregory"

"Thank you Kaitlin. I am here live and on the scene. Local business El Fetche' was once a beautiful building located in the uprising downtown. This building was adored by many since it was literally wall to wall windows. You may have passed it a time or two if you walked the neighborhood. The bottom part of the building contained a safe room that was not originally listed on the blue prints of the business. Right now local authorities are onsite now taming the damaging fire.

The safe room contained the fire for the most part however the fire department had to enter the building from the rear where some of the windows had broken. So far there haven't been any casualties reported however things are still early in this developing story." "Goodness, Gregory. You be safe out there and we will check in on you later. For now we will revert our attention to the weather report and sports right after this break. Be prepared to hear who is in rehab this week." Kaitlin took the show out to a break. I was so nervous. This fire didn't take place too much longer after I left.

I wonder if they will request any of the security footage leading up to this disaster. Could I be a suspect? I shouldn't be, if they do run back the tape it will show me being thrown out on my butt. I had no need to worry there. Right now I was so comfortable about my safety. I walked around in my silk black robe. I liked to switch things up a little. I generally change robes from room to room. It would give me a whole vibe. I got up and still began to pack a bag. I thought I was in the clear but you never know.

I needed to at least see the end part of the news just in case they find anyone hurt. I grabbed a few pair of jeans out of the wardrobe and then in the middle of the commercial about feeding the children another breaking news flash came up. "Right now you are seeing live footage on the scene of El Fetche'. We are seeing movement coming from the building. Officers are assisting the medical response team." I stood directly in front of the television.

My eyes were glued. I didn't want to blink. I was too scared to miss something. There was a crowd surrounding the building, but the camera man was able to get a few good frames. There were two gurneys rolled out and the bodies were in black bags. The last gurney had someone on it but they were covered with several blankets. It looked like a body bag but I couldn't tell. My mind was blown, I felt it in my spirit someone was dead. My mind was racing trying to determine who could have been left behind. I couldn't bare to watch anymore.

I turned off the T.V. and laid back on the bed. I searched through my cell phone for numbers to employees that where still in the building. It dawned on me when I was being thrown out, someone asked for a security sweep. I did my best to log into my app for El Fetche' but it wouldn't load. I had been ghosted by the company. I was sick to my stomach. My anxiety was starting to give me options on how to get my contacts. Everyone knows when you are taken away in the ambulance they will take you to the nearest hospital.

I hopped up and stuffed more clothes in my bag. I walked over to my closet and pushed the mirror to the side. My clothes were color coordinated. I was feeling like a ninja. I needed to slip in and out. I saw a pair of black Levi Jeans that were calling my name. I knew I had a drawer full of black tee's. I closed my closet door and proceeded to slide the other mirror. My shoes sat neatly aligned. My eyes instantly zoomed in on a pair of black Timberland boots. All I needed was a hoodie and ball cap to hide my face.

I knew it was risky walking into an emergency room looking like a robber but they see all kind of people. If someone stops me I will pretend I am lost. I had to try to see Nina, I just know she was in the room. My bag was packed and I was a few minutes away from being dressed. I did mental run down on everything I might need. I only packed enough for a month.

Most of my jeans and a few favorite shirts. I was going to walk out the house with at least two rolling suitcases. It may be too much to carry when you go on the run. I wasn't used to this life. Felecia would try to pull me in and sometimes I would buckle. Other times, I stood strong to gut feeling majority of the time. Jas would bring me into the mix when there was money to be made. Being on the run wasn't for me.

I needed to do something to get back on the team or someone needs to pay me for my silence. My sympathies for anyone who were hurt in this fire but maybe I can take this and use it to my advantage. I was hoping Rico would be one of the people who were hurt. The world would be too much like right if that were to happen. I replayed the things I was introduced to working for the company. I decided to make a few demands on my way to the hospital. I also figured me threatening them would put me in a better position to relocate. I saved some money over the course of my time with El Fetche'.

My thoughts were digging deeper and deeper into themselves. I tended to overthink and internally stress about things I couldn't control. I knew it was something I would probably need medication for in the future but right now wasn't the time to think about myself. I gathered the rest of my items and I decided to leave behind my bachelorette pad. I am hoping to return to it one day. If I played my cards right I could return with a lot more than what I am leaving with. I had to humble myself over my lifetime. I remember the day I met Nina. She hosted a private event at a dope cabin. Nothing but money was in the building. I was there because of Felecia and her vendetta against Nina. I was on payroll to unlock all doors that where attached to the kitchen.

There were supposed to be a few pop up guest throughout the night. Things began to escalate throughout the night. I was entertained. I was half naked walking around serving people drinks and items they may need from the kitchen. Some asked for melted chocolate and others asked for whip cream. I didn't judge, I was living the life in that moment. People were everywhere lusting over each other.

I had died and gone to heaven. Some of the pop up guest began to show up one by one. They would find their cheating spouses and things went to hell in a hand basket quick. The host was no where to be found at the time until we all heard a loud noise. Someone had a gun and wasn't afraid to use it. That part of the evening was unexpected. We all began to panic. Moments later we heard the door open and everyone rushed for the exit. I knew this was exactly what Felecia wanted. She wanted chaos. It was unfolding right before my eyes. Suddenly, the chaos began to simmer down, I heard the music again. I looked around and there she was. Nina. Dancing seductively. If I had a real penis I know I would have a hard on. Nonetheless, she was coming my way. She was beautiful.

Her body moved like it was singing its own song. I was mesmerized along with everyone else in the room. The doors were all closed and the attention was on the Goddess in the room. Nina was beyond perfect. She locked eyes with me and began to approach me. At first I thought I was possibly in the way of someone else. I moved to the side to get out of her path. I was a butler girl , holding a tray with drinks and dildo's. It was like our bodies were in sync. She moved everywhere I moved.

She looked at the tray I was holding and some random person took the tray from my hands. My mind was blown because I didn't sign up for this. I had a girlfriend at the time. Jasmyn, who was Felecia's best friend. I had a brief thought of her and it quickly vanished the moment Nina made contact with me. She smelled so good. Not like perfume good. It was more of a fresh good. We danced until the party got on track. That night once everything calmed down I was asked to come to an after party with Nina and Tae. I was game.

They flaked on me, at the time I didn't realize they only juiced me for information. From that day forward, I was hooked. I walked into the ER and bypassed the information desk. I kept my head down and slid into the back where they housed patients. I saw Rico standing at the edge of a bed so I hid in the room beside him. He was on the phone. I heard him say there were two casualties and one in critical condition. I heard someone approaching. It was Nina. She was alive. Thank God, she was alive. I took a deep breath and knocked over the trashcan. I stumbled. Someone cleared their throat. I turned to face the door. It was Rico. I almost defecated on myself. He saw me and it was no turning back now. I was pissed. My plan was over. Mission failed.

Chapter 8 – Rolinda

Things had gotten a little out of hand in the situation room. We were all under pressure to get our side of the stories heard. For the most part I remained silent, just observing. You get to see people true colors when you simply sit in silence. I had a lot of drinks while we were there. I didn't lose my cool but I can't say the same for the others involved. I had my own demons and skeletons scratching to bust out the closet.

We all walked away with an understanding of releasing El Fetche' from ever being responsible for this case. Nina made it clear how we would move forward. I snuck out the door once Tae began to go on another rampage. Things quickly went left and I could only imagine the results of her madness. Being in the same room with Emjay's father was hard for me especially when everything was laid out on the table. He was a real monster. We have had a few rough nights in the past.

He would ask me to dress up and do certain things I had never experienced. He had his own issues for sure but discovering everything about him only makes me wonder how my son would come out. He was his father so those same traits are in him. I didn't want Emjay to turn into his father. This is not the life I see him in. In the past we have had to remove Emjay from school. He was originally in public school but he had an issue with a Caucasian girl. Well, it was a few, he was smart and bright. I didn't mind making different arrangements for him.

He needed to be away from some of the things I have been involved in over the course of the last year. This weekend when he comes home, I plan to tell my sister the truth. How can I expect my son to be the best him he could be when I am surrounded by nothing but lies and life changing secrets. I was responsible for his life. I was sitting in the kitchen making myself a midnight snack when my phone began to ring. I asked my Google to answer the call. It was Rico, he was yelling. I could hear sirens in the background. My speakers were loud. The kitchen was filled with whatever chaos he was surrounded by. I asked him what was going on and he didn't respond. I could hear him talking to someone in the background.

They were on the way to the hospital. I didn't know if I should hang up on stay on the line. I started to get scared for a moment but decided to keep my composure. I needed to take out my note pad and jot down everything I hear. I didn't know if he was in danger or not. I grabbed the pen off the magnet holder on the fridge. I did my best to hear what he was saying. Everything sounded muffled. I decided to hang up. I quickly ran up the steps to my room. I tossed on some yoga pants and a tank top.

I was anticipating another call from Rico. I dialed Nina's number to see if she was available to fill me in on what was happening. It didn't take long for her to answer. "Roe?" She said. "Nina? Is everything ok?" I asked. I was nervous. Nina began to explain she was at the hospital getting checked out. She also said she had to speak with the police. She wanted to make sure I could meet them down at the station once she is discharged. I told her I didn't mind meeting her downtown. I asked if she wanted to talk about it, she said she barely knows what to say. She sounded like she was going through something.

Hopefully she would be willing to talk about it when I see her. I couldn't represent her if she didn't tell me what was going on. I didn't want to be blindsided, but I had to trust her enough to not put me in that type of predicament. It didn't take long before I was in the car heading to the station. I made sure to bring my brief case with me. I wouldn't say I was dressed as a professional lawyer at this time, but I think we would all agree I can get a pass due to the circumstances.

I heard my phone vibrating. This time it wasn't a call, it was a text message. "Are you ok?" It was from my sister. Tati hadn't reached out to me since we had our little conversation. I responded back through an audio clip. "Nice of you to check in on me. How are you?" I asked being smug. I noticed she was typing. There were the small dots at the bottom of the messages.

I put the phone down after a few moments. I gathered myself as I pulled into the station. I was still wondering what this could be about. It was my job to help play nice. I don't know if I was in the mood for that but I was going to do the best I could. It didn't take long before I was walking through the metal detector. I was being escorted to an interview room. The hallway was dim and creepy. If they were using intimidation tactics on people I'm sure it works.

I am glad to be on the other side of things, but it is still uncomfortable. The officer opened the door for me. Nina was sitting at the table with a look of defeat on her face. There was an officer on the other side of the table. He looked more like a detective since he wasn't in the normal uniform. I was disheveled by this entire vibe. Nina cleared her throat as if she was telling me to hurry up and get her out of here.

I remained standing and the now confirmed detective introduced himself. "Hello, I'm detective Roger Watson. Thank you for joining us." He said as he extended his hand to greet me. "Hello, I am Rolinda Taylor, representation for Nina Toussaint. These are odd business hours. I hope we can make this quick. I am sure my client is more than ready to go home." I said as I extended my hand in return. He flashed his white teeth and began to take a seat.

He was brown skinned, shorter than the average man. He looked like a complete nerd. I had no idea how he made detective. His suit was practically falling off him along with his glasses. Poor thing looked overworked and underpaid. I smiled and took my seat. I was eager to hear why we were here. I began to remove my notepad and pen from my bag as Mr. Watson began to share with me the reason we are here.

I leaned over to Nina and asked if she was ok and if she would like to have something to drink. Nina smiled noticing I was completely ignoring Mr. Watson. I didn't know how long she had been here. It was imperative as a paid representative. Mr. Watson noticed I was no longer listening and paused for a moment. He smiled and pushed his glasses up on his face. He simply crossed his hands and waited silently. I started to feel uncomfortable because we could feel him staring a hole in the side of our heads. I turned and asked him to bring in two glasses of water before we get started.

I expected him to become flustered but instead he shook his head in agreeance and smiled. He pushed himself back in the chair and walked out the door. Nina turned back towards me and began to talk. I held my finger up to her lips. I quickly advised her ninety percent of the time these conversations are recorded. I also explained I would need to ask for actual privacy to speak with you. She looked at me with sadness in her eyes.

I began to regret asking the detective to leave maybe we should hurry this up. I grabbed her hand and lightly squeezed it. Our silence was interrupted when Mr. Watson returned holding three bottles of water and a few packs of crackers. I was pleased with his chivalry. He distributed the bottles of water and laid the packs of crackers in the middle of the table.

He fixed his tie and asked if it was alright for him to continue. Nina and I both nodded our heads in agreeance. Mr. Watson continued. This time he allowed his photos to speak for themselves. He slowly removed photos from a scene that looked like it had been torched. I looked at Nina who wouldn't make eye contact with me. Mr. Watson laid so many photos on the table they were starting to fall onto the floor. I made eye contact with the detective who was seemingly enjoying himself as his smile was no longer bright but sinister.

I think I may have underestimated him. I was a thousand percent intrigued. So I dove right in and assisted with the placing of the photos . As I combed through them, I noticed a few familiar items. It was photos of El Fetche. Things began to turn sideways when the photos went from burned material from the room our meeting was held in to bodies. I took a deep breath as soon as I saw the distortion of a lifeless body laying at what looked like to be the door of the room.

It was almost like they were trying to make it out. I did my best to contain my thoughts. The room itself was silent until Nina burst into tears. I hadn't noticed he was holding a new photo. It was a toe tag that was written out for Tae. I grabbed Nina's hand and this time I held it tightly. My heart was breaking for her. They were more than friends. They were legit family. I loved their bond. It was authentic to the tee.

I shed a tear myself before turning to the detective. I had to snap out of these emotions. "So, is there a question in all of this?" I asked. It was obvious this presentation of photos was overwhelming. "I'm glad you asked Miss Taylor. Can you explain why the prestigious El Fetche ended up in flames?" He asked now removing his jacket. Nina looked at me and I nodded my head advising it was ok to answer. I also gave her the eye to ensure she knew not to say too much just in case she was involved. "I am unsure as to what took place in the meeting area once I left. Things were resolved and I ended the meeting."

Nina said through her tears. I on the other hand decided to gather the photos and place them in a stack next to him. I wanted to remove the dreadful images of the tragedy that has taken place. Once I was done with organizing things to my liking. I did my best to end this hunt for my client. "Well, she has answered your question. Is there anything else you need before I take my client home. These photos you have displayed tonight are unbelievably vile. It is clear my client is in no shape to continue this interview.

We will continue to be cooperative as we too would like to know what has happened. However, as you have shown us one of her closest friends was involved. I think that alone should allow us the opportunity to reschedule." I didn't take a breath. I needed to get her out of here. This was a lot for me to process but I can only imagine what Nina is going though. I had so many questions but this was not the space to have that conversation. "Here's the thing, I don't believe you have played a part in this incident at this time.

However I do expect you to cooperate as this is an ongoing investigation." He said. Still ignoring my concerns. I decided to take it upon myself to stand. I looked down at Nina and let her know it was ok to do the same. I thanked the nice detective for his time and we walked out the room and made our way to the exit. I was feeling confident Nina was telling the truth. Knowing Tae is no longer with us, was the main factor on ruling her out. She would never bring any harm to her. We walked out of the station and quickly hopped into my car.

Once inside I locked the doors and hugged her for what seemed like ages. She was still crying. She was hurting. Once we ended our embrace, I squeezed her hand once more letting her know I was here for her. I asked if she had someone, she wanted me to call. She shook her head. I started the car and we began our journey home. The radio was off. Nina was no longer crying. She was staring out of the window. Nina lived on the outskirts of the city so we had a ways to go. I asked her to pull the eye glass case out the glove compartment. She reached and found the item. She opened them assuming she would find something. She did. It was a nice treat to puff on while we traveled. She looked at me and smiled. "Girl. You know me so well." She said and we laughed in unison as she lit up. I decided to let her get a few pulls in before I picked her brain. Moments later she was passing me the peace stick. It was now or never. We still had a pretty good distance to travel so it was perfect timing. "Nina, what happened honey?"

I asked in the sincerest voice I could muster up. Nina was big on tones. So I had to ensure I presented the topic with grace. "So what happened?" I asked. She hung her head low. I passed her the smoke. I know she needed it more than I did. It was a lot to digest. "It's been a long night." She laughed surprisingly as she took a long pull off the peace stick. "So you know after we left out the situation room I was ready to go home. I went to my office to make note of the final decision I shared with everyone prior to leaving.

I was sitting at the computer and time got away from me to be honest. We made sure Jodi got out the building but other than that everything was normal. Rico left for the night and I was packing things up to go." She paused for a moment. Took two quick puffs and passed it back to me.

As she exhaled, she continued. "I was on my way out the door when I saw smoke creeping from under the door of the situation room." Everything from that point is a blur. I do remember going to the hospital to be checked out. Rico was with me. He saw Jodi and disappeared. I was glad he did because that's when Detective Watson showed up to asked me questions." She hung her head low once more. We were still far away from her place. I didn't want to pressure her to say anything else. I get it. She was more than hurt. Everything is in an uproar.

I had to know though, I needed to know who all made it out. "Who all was left?" I asked clinching my teeth. I felt horrible digging for the tea but I still needed to know so I could be prepared for Mr. Watson. I glanced over and noticed she was crying again. I took a free hand and grabbed her a napkin out of the side of my door. Every black female keep a stash of napkins in her car. I handed her the tissue and she apologized for being a mess. She went on to explain who was left in the situation room, she also questioned Sonjay's whereabouts.

It was clear when he left, his anger was high. He was probably upset because of the decisions Nina made regarding the case. I was with her on the low. He would benefit the most from Kyle no longer living. If he did do something before, he left the room, I can only image if he would go after Jess or Jasmyn whatever her name is. I broke the weird silence and asked if she wanted to crash at my place for a while just until she feels better. She nodded her head. I still wanted to take her to her house.

I am sure she would want to pack a few bags. We rode In silence the rest of the ride. A little under an hour of sitting beside a bear and we were finally pulling up to her place. It was beautiful. I thought she only had a condo in the city but apparently this place was secret and off in the cut. I couldn't help but give her props. I parked in the drive way and a staff member opened my door. Before exiting I tapped her on the leg and let her know she was home. It took a few taps but eventually she woke up.

She smiled looking at her staff as the gentleman proceeded to open the door. It was clear she had a thing for Cubans. As we walked up the walkway to her door we passed four more staff members who greeted us as we passed. She punched in her pin and the door unlocked. Nina was living her best life. I wasn't mad at her for it. Once we walked through the entrance my jaw hit the floor. Her house was even more beautiful on the inside. Her home was breathtaking. Everything was white and gold. It totally had an open space concept. There were more windows than there were walls. It felt so airy, and it smelled like I was walking through heaven; it felt like pure peace. Shoot I needed to be asking her if I can just stay with her. I laughed to myself yet again another Cuban was waiting with a huge smile on his face.

He was a chocolate Cuban. I needed to place an order for a set to watch over me. I mean my house. Nina left me standing in the main entrance looking around the room in amazement. I could hear her yelling from the top of the stairs. She was inviting me upstairs. I snapped out of my trance and the bell boy grabbed my hand to lead me to my destination. I was obviously in heat. I did my best to make sure my feet moved in unison as we were almost to the top.

Once I placed my foot on the last step the bell boy held my arm to secure my stance an turned around quickly disappearing once more to retake his post. Nina was standing in her closet packing her suitcase. From the looks of it she planned on moving in. She just had to grab the biggest suitcase she had. She still looked exhausted. It dawned on me that I too was drained emotionally but would still have to drive back into town to get to my house. I walked in the closet and asked if I could help her pack. She ignored my question and began to talk about Tae. She was on her heart as expected.

I saw a place to sit and I allowed her to simply vent. She was still packing as she talked. I didn't speak a word. She needed this and I knew what it was to feel empty after losing a friend. She was asking if I remembered when we all first met. We were in Bora Bora. It was weird meeting two strangers and making close bonds in a matter of seven days. We had a ball. Tati and I were there on a spiritual breakthrough. Nina and Tae where there for the same kind of energy. Nina moved on to another topic.

This time explaining how Rico and Tae would butt heads back in the day. She laughed as she grabbed a few more items from the dresser. She was obviously in a state where she was just not present. We were in her closet way too long. I did my best to hurry things on letting her know we can come back for more if she wanted to. Just as I was getting her to wrap up this delightful packing session her phone rang. It was sitting on a solar charger.

We both froze. It continued to ring. I realized I needed to check my phone. Nina reached for her phone and answered, I figured she might need some alone time. I walked out of the closet and back into what seemed to be a bathroom. It was just as flawless as everything else in the house. I pulled out my cell phone to see if I had any missed calls. My son along with Jay had called me. That was weird. I reached out to MJ first and there was no response. I hit Jay back and he picked up after two rings. "Roeeeee." He said as answered. That was usually code for- my wife is around.

I asked him why he was calling me and if he had heard from MJ. He cleared his throat and kept the same energy. "Yeah, umm MJ is here with Tati. We were worried because he came home and realized you were not there. He called and Tati sent him a car and brought him here. We just wanted to let you know your kid is safe." He said. The last part caught me off guard. His tone changed a bit. It went from I am a fun uncle to a disappointed father. It pissed me off to be honest.

I found another sitting stool I could plop down on while I gave Jay the business. "Listen dead beat. It's not my kid, its OUR kid and honestly I think it is about time to let it all be known." I said noticing my reflection in the ceiling to wall mirror. My face was scrunched up and my lips were so far in the air I was surprised I was breathing. I took a deep breath and had a silent laugh of how quickly this man can get under my skin. I got back to the topic at hand. "I am glad he is ok, I will have to get him tomorrow if that is cool with you. I am working a case right now." I said letting him know MJ will always be my number one priority. Furthermore, I don't understand why my sister didn't simply call me. Why did Jay have to deliver the news?

I was frustrated and the day had simply slipped out of my hands. I was beyond pissed that Tati didn't give me a call. I guess she in her feelings yet again about whatever comes in her mind. Jay ended the call without responding as if I was nothing. Complete trash. I wanted to toss the phone across the room but I chose not to. I was in someone else's house and I was not going to come here and show out. I made a mental note to check in on Tati later.

We were too old to keep doing the same ol same ol. Come to think about it, I realized there could be more to this story. I jumped up immediately heading back into Nina's closet. She wasn't there. I called her name but not too loudly because I knew she had taken a phone call. Who knows if she was still on the phone or not? I was ready to get back to my house.

I needed to get my son. I don't want him around anyone who didn't want him around. My head began to hurt as I still wondered around the house. I finally found Nina who was talking to Rico. They were discussing Jodi. I walked in and tapped the door. Rico turned and made eye contact with me. I smiled acknowledging him. Nina looked at me as well. "Hey Roe. I think I am going to go ahead and stay home.

Thank you for helping me this evening. My days are running together. I just need some rest." Nina said as she leaned in and hugged me. I was still making eye contact with Rico as I am most positive, he is the reason of her changing her mind. I smiled and told her it was ok and I would let myself out. Before turning to leave I asked Nina if she could give me details on the security company, she uses to man her house. She tapped Rico on the shoulder and said I would need to chat with him. I replied maybe at another time, I made my exit and took my time walking down the staircase.

The same bell boy was waiting to assist me with the last step. He opened the door for me and I was on my own again. I had to travel back home with nothing but space and opportunity to think about my life and the direction I should be taking. One thing was clear, Jay had pissed me off to the point of no return. I was over the bull crap and if Nina can forgive Rico for faking his death then I should be able to be forgiven for having an affair with my sisters husband.

Tonight was the night I planned to once again let it all out. This time I think she should know everything. I know it would be a hard pill to swallow but my son needed his father and not temporarily but permanently. It was time he told her how he felt. I typed in my sisters address in my GPS. It would take me no time to eat up the highway.

My adrenaline was pumping. I reached over and grabbed another peace stick out of my stash. Instead of riding in silence I decided turn all the way up. I reached in the back and felt around for the netted pouch on the seat. It took me a few minutes but I was able to pull out an airplane bottle of Hennessey.

I liked to have a party pack with me sometimes. I know with me being a lawyer it is risky but I have my days of irresponsibility and lets just say I am in the mood. I am tired of being tossed to the side like I'm nothing. Lizzo was playing on my phone so I connected it to the Bluetooth. I was riding in the wind.

It was late and the roads are clear. I didn't run into any congestion until I arrived at Tati's house. There was a line of cars parked at her street. I guess someone was having a party. I had to park so far away. I ended up walking up the hill wondering why the heck people where

here. I tried to find the house were the party was but I didn't hear any music. In fact it was really quiet. Once I made it to the door step I was out of breath. To be honest the cuss out I had planned in my head had suddenly faded. I could hear voices from behind the door.

I rang the door bell. It didn't take long before MJ was opening the door. "Mama, come in aunt Tati is having a party." He said full of excitement. I smiled and gave him a big hug. I missed my baby. I was holding him so tight and it was interrupted by Jay. "Hey you two, come in and shut the door. I don't want any bugs getting in."

There he was. standing in front of me. I had a thing or two I needed to get off my chest. I was stuck. It was something about the man that melted me into a puddle instantly. He went around us and shut the door. He placed his hand on the bottom of my back and guided us into the living room. There were people everywhere. Standing and conversing with one another.

I hadn't realized she was throwing an event but then I saw her sitting on the sofa. She looked horrible. What is going on here. I realized people were not laughing. In fact everyone was sulking. Jay released me and joined Tati on the sofa. I still had my arm around MJ and I whispered to him. I wanted to know why there were so many people in the house and what was wrong with Tati? MJ explained she was informed her aunt Tyesha was killed in the fire at my job. My heart sunk.

Here I was making sure my client was taken care of and lusting over her staff when I should have been finding out the other victims. In that moment it hit me. She was grieving. Just hours ago she was told her best friend was no longer living. We all grew up together. They were more like sisters than we were. I was always jealous of them as a kid. More memories flooded my mind.

It was overwhelming to be honest. I couldn't imagine what Tati was going through. I also still couldn't understand why there were so many people here. Jay was holding Tati's hand and MJ was no longer standing beside me. I was not about to sit in this room of sorrow. I walked over to Tati and grabbed her hand.

She quickly removed herself from the couch. It was like she wanted to get away from everyone just as I did. We walked through to the kitchen. There were boxes of chicken and jugs of sweet tea everywhere. Money didn't mean shy away from certain traditions. In the event a black family Is mourning for someone people come from all over to pay their respect. It is almost as if it is the circle of life.

The village steps in and provides food and anything you may need at that time. In a few days the hype will calm down and we will still be left with broken hearts and wilted boxes of chicken. I didn't want to use this space. We kept walking until I reached the sliding door. Once outside I stopped and held on to her as tight as I could.

She reciprocated in return. I couldn't let her go. We both just whaled for a few minutes. We finally released each other and began to wipe each others eyes. What happened?'' I asked as she took a tissue and dabbed my nose. "I don't know. It's an investigation taking place now. You were there right? Tati told me about a meeting she was taking. We were working on the case with Jay and Kyle." I rolled my eyes as soon as she mentioned Jay. "Yeah. I was there. Then Nina ended the meeting once the decision was made on how we would all move forward. Some of us left one behind the other.

Kyle and Ty were discussing things that had come out over the course of the evening." I told her everything I remembered as far as who was left behind, it went silent and all I could hear was crickets. I began to get quick flashbacks of what I learned Jay had been up to. I remembered why I was here in the first place other than collecting MJ. "I'll be back." I told Tati. I opened the door and went to address the guest who were still mingling.

"Excuse me." I said. Allowing a few moments for the chatter to stop. "Thank you all for being here. It has been a long day and our family just needs a little time to grieve. Please feel free to take home any of the items on the table. We greatly appreciate you for coming." I smiled and pivoted towards the kitchen. It was like a stampede was coming behind me.

I crept out the door and joined Tati. We stood outside watching the same people who brought us food tearing through it like a pack of wild animals. We laughed so hard. I hadn't noticed we were holding hands until the laughter stopped. Tati was bundled up in her blanket squeezing my hand. I thought now was as good time as any to let it out. "I got something to tell you." I said.

I blurted it out so quickly. The moment it released my lips I wanted to take it back. "You can tell me anything." Tati said, now taking her attention from the kitchen and placing it on me. I turned to face her and I grabbed her other hand. I stared into her face. I saw she was already going through it but I couldn't take it anymore. Jay was a major creep and honestly I was no better. "Tati. . . I . I don't even know where to start." I said "I told you. You have been tripping Roe. What's up?" She asked. I released her hands and walked over to the gazebo. "Jay is a joke." I said.

"What do you mean? What he do now." She asked tossing her hands in the air headed in my direction. "Well, you know I can't tell you details of the case I am working or was working. I don't know what is happening now." I said. "The case with Kyle and Jay? It is so sad that Kyle was like that. I never thought I would have to add rapist to his character."

Her face looked disgusted. "Ty didn't deserve that. She was worth more." She hung her head low. "Your right she did. So do you Tati. You deserve more." I said. Screw it the gloves where off. It just is what it is at this point. "

Look Tati, Jay has been a pig to both me and you. I am sorry to tell you this but Jay is MJ's father." I said but before I could continue Tati slapped me in the face. "Tati. Let me…" Smack!! I didn't want to hit her back. She was pushing me over and over yelling. The neighbors light came on. "Let's go in the house sis I know you're mad but we can talk inside."

I said taking a quick walk back inside the house. She was right on my heels, yelling and asking questions. I pulled out my phone and ordered MJ a car so he could go home. It would be here in fifteen minutes so I had time to get Tati to calm down. "Aye!!" I yelled before we walked in. "You can be mad, I get it but control yourself while my son is here. Give me twenty minutes and he will be gone and we can talk then." I said. I meant every word. Tati knew I didn't play that around MJ.

I preferred to keep him out of my personal business. She stopped shouting and pushed past me. She shoved me into the glass door. Tati was beyond pissed. She was hurt and had every right to be. I reluctantly walked in behind her. I was hanging my head low. I reached the living room where Jay was sitting on the couch in the same space. The site of him felt like it gave me an ulcer. MJ must have been upstairs, which was perfect. Tati reached the living room before I did and her face hadn't changed. It was still distorted. She sat down beside Jay.

I choose to stand by the stairs so I can watch for MJ's car. Tati's foot was shaking so fast. She usually did that when she was upset. I could hear her starting to mumble under her breath. I knew she couldn't hold it in much longer. Before I knew it, she was asking Jay questions about the case. I sat down on the steps. I didn't want to be in the room with them. I wanted to disappear. "So what part did you play in Kyles case Sonjay?"

Tati asked. When she used his full name in an argument it was going to heat up based on his responses. I wanted to pop up from the staircase and spill all the tea but MJ's car was outside. My phone just went off. "MJ!"

I yelled. It didn't take long before we heard stomping from upstairs. It sounded like he fell but I didn't want to put him on blast. I laughed as he skipped a few steps to reach the bottom. I gave him a kiss and told him I would be home soon. He ran over to kiss Tati and Sonjay good night. I closed the door once he hopped in the car. I texted him and told him to let me know when he was in the house.

Once the door was closed Tati was back on her feet. "Jay?" Is there something you want to tell me?" Tati asked as she dipped off into the kitchen. Sonjay looked at me confused. There was a lot he needed to tell her but I doubt it will happen. He was a dirty dog. I know I was wrong for being upset but I had feelings for him, I wasn't just any random side piece. He was the father of my child. I heard rambling in the kitchen.

Jay had yet to answer the question. He was still looking at me as if I would give him a clue as to what he should be admitting to. Tati returned from the kitchen holding a knife. She was low key crazy now, add grieving and betrayal to the list and you have toxic Tati. I ran over and stood in front of her. I was not going to allow her to lose her cool and catch a charge.

"Please Tati just listen." I begged her with my arms held up and my back facing her. I was the only thing keeping her from handcuffs. "What is going on here. Why is she so angry Roe?" He asked. Looking at me for answers. I stared him down and, in that moment, he knew why Tati was exploding. He had the nerve to look at me as if he was hurt. I removed myself from in between them. Tati agreed to sit down and hear us out. I thanked her. I apologized and spilled my guts.

When I was done the sun was coming up and it was yet again another sleepless night. Tati was sitting on the couch still silent. Her tears were no longer streaming down her face. She had the look in her eyes. She was numb. Respectfully so. I knew she needed a moment to let it all sink in. Tonight, had been a lot for all of us I am sure. I stood and told them I had to get back to MJ. I kissed Tati on her forehead, walked towards the door. Before I left, Tati spoke. "Roe. Let this be the last time you walk through that door."

Her words were sharper than the knife held earlier. I turned to see if she was kidding. However, she brushed passed me and went up the stairs. Sonjay stood up and grabbed the crystal doves on the coffee table and tossed it against the wall. As I shut the door behind me I knew it would be the last time I talked to my sister. Was I wrong for telling her. I thought it would make me feel better to stop living a lie.

Now I feel a lot worse than I did before. What is life? What am I going to do? We don't have family it is just us for the most part. I walked slowly to my car. I looked back to see if she was even going to watch me walk away. Instead I could see the shadow of them arguing upstairs. I was a home wrecker. Everything was falling apart. Nothing will be the same anymore.

I backed out the drive way with a heavy heart. The sun was bright, and my eyes were puffy from crying. I didn't want to hear any music I just wanted to be home in a blink of an eye.

Chapter 9: Jess / Jasmyn

I have been patiently waiting to hear from Sonjay dusty self. I should have known he would take his time with paying me. Nina word didn't mean anything, and I was a fool to agree to the terms she set. I wasn't satisfied, she hadn't paid enough for me to feel better about the death of my best friend. Felecia was my only family. I had to hold her down. I know she would do the same for me. The same Cubans that were after me were probably the same ones who killed her.

I know Nina had something to do with that. She can never take responsibility for the sneaky things she do. I have tried to take her down and every turn it never works out. She was Batman and I was the joker. I saw on the news things heated up a bit at El Fetche. I wonder what happened. I did my best to pay off staff to be whistle blowers but they always folded. Obviously, all I needed was liquor and a cigarette. I called Jodi earlier to see if she wanted to hash things out but it was clear she was still on her high horse.

I was disappointed I thought we would always ride off into the sunset. She didn't recognize me at first because of my surgeries. I wanted a new identity. I couldn't show up thinking everyone would have open arms. Sonjay on the other hand never knew what hit him. I knew he was still a killer and if he didn't pay up the world will know as well. I sat in bed on my laptop looking for sightings of Sonjay. I needed to see what he was up to.

I couldn't find anything so far and I have been logged into social media for hours. I sent a text out to Jodi but she hadn't responded. I had no other moves to make. I needed to figure out where Sonjay was and Nina. I couldn't call my lawyer. I was left out back as usual without anything. I was so lost and this is how I always am without Felicia.

She would have had the back up plan ready to go. Me on the other hand tried my best to come up with something. I needed her more now than ever. I got out of bed and walked over to the window. It was peaceful to look out on to the city. It hit me. Things are hot right now because of the fire at El Fetche.

I had the perfect idea that would turn this fire situation into a full-on blaze. I was intrigued with the fact that I could come up with something so conniving. Felecia would be proud. I wanted to make sure I had my new ducks in a row. I stopped wasting time and hopped on the bed and started searching for what I needed. Before you know it, I found the perfect lead. I rushed to get dressed, it didn't take long before I was rushing out the door heading to get things turned up. I was close to the city so I knew once I combed through traffic I would be there.

It didn't take more than twenty minutes before I was sitting in front of the news station. I found the perfect reporter who only covered fashion. I wanted to make sure I gave an interview to someone who may need the come up. Plus, she was the only black reporter on the crew. So of course, I had to make sure I tossed her a bone. Her email was online, and I already warned her I was en-route. She responded quickly right before exiting the highway letting me know to walk across the street to the coffee shop beside the station. I didn't mind meeting her there. It was probably better to be in a laid-back environment. I checked my face prior to exiting the car.

I looked both ways before running across the street to the quant (quaint?)café. I felt like I was a damsel in destress. I knew I was making the best decision. It didn't take long before I was opening the door to a major come back in this game. There she was. Sitting in the back of the shop in the second to last booth close to the bathroom. I had to admit this was a little far fetched to be so close to the bathroom but hey I had plenty of time to teach my new friend how to have some class even when its something juicy being served on the table. She waved her hand to acknowledge I was in the right place. I had to admit, tv added ten pounds on her. It did her no justice. Her brown chocolate complexion was appetizing. She was conformed to being on camera.

Her hair was relaxed with a part down the middle. Her eyes were hazel, and her smile could use some work. Nonetheless I wasn't here to marry the girl I just wanted to tell my truth. I sat down and reached my hand out to introduce myself. We made our pleasantries. An awkward silence passed and the waitress came over to take our order. We gazed at the menu for a moment and then placed our orders. "Well, Mrs. Fletcher Fischer?

You called me here today to talk about the pending investigation of the fire that took place just days ago at El Fetche headquarters." She was eager to get the details and I was willing to spill, I was the one who will direct this meeting. "Well, Miss. India Lee. In the flesh. I would hope with the amount of facts I am going to drop on you over the course of …..well…whenever I say… you would at least allow a girl the courtesy to get to know you a tad. " I said. I was in control. I needed her to know that. Her response was vague and laughed it off. I was assuming she thought I was playing.

"Ok. Then ask away." She replied. "Now that I have your attention, I would like to know in what ways can you help me?" I asked. She was straight forward from the gate so I returned the pleasantries. "I mean you called me, I would assume being on television would be enough." She said as she cocked her head to the side. I was starting to see why the station kept her from the lime light.

She didn't have any personable skills. She was basic. The one percenter that is hired for quota. I laughed it off and reached in my bag to pull out my demands. Just as we were about to really get down to business our food showed up. India looked relieved. We both smiled as the waitress placed our plates down in front of us. I asked for a cup of coffee and water to go with my meal. India ordered the same.

Once the waitress walked off India held her hands out and began to pray over her food. I was taken aback for a moment trying to figure out when was the last time I had done that. India's tone was soft and compassionate. "Lord, We are gathered here today to fellowship over a freshly prepared meal. May this meeting give us both satisfaction and please bless the hands that prepared this lovely meal. Amen" I simply joined in on the back end like most non-believers.

I said Amen at the completion of the prayer. I was so ready to dig into my flap jacks. I still wanted to remain focused on the task at hand. I cut my pancake. I chewed for a moment before getting back into the thick of things. "Before our food arrived you were just about to let me know in what ways you can be of assistance to me." I asked. No need to drag this thing out. She sat there for a moment swirling her fork around a massive puddle of syrup. She stopped abruptly and listed what she could do for me.

" Since television isn't enough that means you have enough dirt on people to last a lifetime. If you can promise me all exclusive interviews then I am here at your disposal. Now, what I will not do, is anything illegal to jeopardize my brand. We clear?" She asked. I wasn't expecting her to have such an educated response. I was impressed to say the least. I was ok with her terms even though she clearly skipped the question yet again. I was satisfied. She said just what I wanted to hear.

Once she said she was at my full disposal, things felt like they are really aligning. I nodded my head letting her know I can agree to our new found friendship. We spent the rest of the meeting talking and getting on the same page. I was content. It felt right. We made additional arrangements to follow up later at my place. I was thrown off when she asked if my place was a safe space. I didn't mind but I was totally picking up some vibes.

I wouldn't mind exploring options. She was digging some of the tips I was dropping on a few big names around the town. I had her full attention, I guess I will have to find out if it was in more ways than one. We wrapped things up after being there for a little over two hours. She wrote down her task list for following up on a few leads. I left the café feeling empowered.

Just as I was entering my car my phone went off. It was ringing. I couldn't see who was calling so I connected to my Bluetooth. "Hello?" I answered still trying to gather myself before I pulled off. "You not tired of the games yet?" It was an unknown voice. I couldn't catch on to who it was. "Um. You have the wrong number." I said as I pressed the end call button. I cranked the car and buckled up. I wanted to make sure I had things for the evening. India would be coming later this evening, so I had plenty of time to get things set up.

I wanted to share anything I could to bring down Sonjay and more importantly, invincible Nina. Fifteen minutes down the road and my phone was going off again. I allowed the Bluetooth to pick up the line but I said nothing. I didn't want to waste my energy on a prank caller. "How was your meeting?"

I heard the voice say. I still couldn't catch the voice. I thought the first caller was a woman but now it sounds like a soft spoken male. I quickly thought of Sonjay probably trying to scare me off. Before I could respond the caller disconnected the line. I was starting to get a bad feeling in the pit of my stomach. It was almost like I had gas but instead of releasing it, it would roll back up to the top of my stomach. I brushed it off though. What can possibly happen from these calls? I coached myself up as I continued to make my way back home. I reached out to Jodi via text and asked her to come over. I wanted to talk to her. I secretly wanted her to simply be there at the house so I wouldn't be alone.

Reality was, I was alone. There was nothing I can do about that. I wanted to connect with people deeper than I allow myself to. Everyone who I can call on is generally on pay roll for something I need. In other ways I felt there was no need to connect with others. Look at how people are. They do what they want to benefit themselves. I can't say much about that but I am just like them.

My thoughts carried me home. I was still feeling apprehensive inside but couldn't put my finger on it. Jodi finally sent a response saying she would rather not come over. I was pissed to be honest. She acts like what we had was so horrible. She made plenty of money because of me. We should have never allowed her to get in on Nina. It changed her. It was like she was mesmerized and went from catching the bag to working hard for a paycheck. That was her decision.

I parked and sat for a moment. I was frustrated. I knew I had to shake it off and get out my bag. Felecia didn't tell me it was lonely at the top. I gathered my items and headed up to the entrance of my building. I spoke to the gentleman holding the door as I entered. I waited on the elevator. The lobby was bare. Which was unusual. People are standing waiting for the elevator and others are simply coming and going. I was starting to get that feeling again. Just as the bell on the elevator went off I stepped into it.

I was joined by someone just as the doors were closing. I couldn't see their face. It wasn't cold out and yet I was staring at someone who was wearing a black trench coat, a scarf and hat.

I scanned my house card to activate my floor. The weird guy did the same, so I felt better knowing they had a floor to visit. I could only hope they would get off prior to myself. Thank goodness for technology. My floor number will not display or sound off once the floor has been reached. The elevator came to a stop. It was my floor. I was reluctant to exit but I had no other choice. I removed myself slowly from the elevator.

This building was so obvious of how the homes were in the building. There is only one door. I walked slowly trying to allow time for the doors on the elevator to close. I didn't hear any additional footsteps. I turned around before I opened my door just to make sure I was alone. I took a deep breath when no one was behind me. I was being paranoid. I can tell myself those petty phone calls meant nothing but it had me shook.

I was finally home. I entered my alarm code and kicked off my shoes. I had a few more hours before I was having company. I locked the door behind me. I looked around and to see how much damage control needed to be done before the evening got started. I didn't have much to clean up if anything. I was low key excited about that. I sat on the couch and grabbed the laptop sitting on the table. I wanted to browse through a few catering sites to see what I wanted to order.

My phone began to ring this time it was someone facetiming me. It read unknown which was creepy but reluctantly I answered. "How can I help you?" I asked pressing to ignore to approve the screen being shared. There wasn't an answer. I hung up. I decided to turn my phone off for a while. I had no additional energy to play with a prank caller. I asked my Google assistant to set an alarm for three hours from now. I wanted to rest my mind for a while. I walked over to the wine rack and grabbed a bottle. It didn't matter which bottle at this point. I wanted to down the entire bottle. I grabbed a large wine glass from the cabinet. Lucky me, it was large enough to fit the entire bottle. I was happy. I went back over to the laptop and pulled out a few files I was collecting over the time on high profile clients from El Fetche. Last year Felecia and I attempted to take Nina down by attacking her clientele in hopes of them all walking away from the company. That didn't happen. Instead her company was stronger. She was invincible.

They say not to throw stones at a glass house. I thought the glass would break if you did. I was obviously wrong. As I began prepping the information, I promised India, there was a breaking news story on the news. It was more details on the El Fetche fire. Coroners confirmed foul play had taken place prior to the fire. I took a long sip of my wine as the story unfolded. "There have been rumors of foul play and it has been confirmed. The two bodies were found laying by the door of the room were beaten prior to the fire. The male in this incident was unharmed and died of smoke inhalation.

The fire was started by what seemed to be alcohol negligence. The fire started closer to the male victim in the room. We are left to only assume he was the aggressor and killed himself after attacking the other two victims. We will have more on this story as it continues to unfold." The reporter ended the story with a commercial. I was intrigued. I didn't know what took place in the situation room after I left. Kyle must have been pissed about how the evening played out.

Imagine having your wife found out all your dirty secrets right in front of you and there is no way you can turn back the hands of time. It had to be emasculating. Knowing him, he was enraged and snapped because he wasn't getting his way. I can't believe Tae died. What did she have to do with anything? Maybe she was collateral damage. Either way I don't see this story dying down anytime soon. I pulled out my joint and continued pulling together things for the evening. I was debating on making this professional or sensual. I wouldn't mind a perfect combination of both. I finally found a nice restaurant to cater the evening. India looked like the neo soul kind of sister. I think she would be delighted to snack on some Jamaican food. I placed the order and continued to look for my edible plug.

What's a dinner meeting without edibles? I placed all my orders and double checking to make sure they would all arrive on time. I leaned back on the couch and faded off into a deep sleep. I tossed and turned. I was fighting someone and I couldn't see the persons face. It didn't take long before I was on the floor ending what could have been the fight for my life. My buzzer was going off from downstairs.

I quickly dusted myself off. I was lodged between the couch and coffee table. It was tough getting up. I couldn't do anything but laugh once I made it to a good stance. I rushed over to the intercom to see who wanted to be buzzed in. "Hello?" I said, all out of breath. I looked down at my leg to make sure I didn't hurt myself on the way down to the ground. I patiently waited on a response from the lobby but no one answered.

I guess it was a random person looking to get anyone to let them in. I checked the time and I had slept forty minutes past the time I needed to. I hated feeling like I was under pressure. I had to hurry up and get things ready for the evening. I dashed back over to my laptop and checked the status of the food delivery. I turned my phone back on to see if I had any messages.

I apparently was still tuned in to the local news station but there were no alarming reports as of now. I was content even though I was running behind the original schedule I set for myself. As my phone came on it began to vibrate multiple times. I didn't want to look at it but just like everyone else who hear that phone go off- its like an itch you got to scratch. I grabbed my phone, still refusing to look at it and headed towards my bathroom. I was ready for a shower to really get me in the mood to entertain tonight. I placed my phone into the holder attached in the shower. I connected it to the Bluetooth speaker. Before I hopped in the shower I scrolled through my text. It wasn't anything alarming just the usual DM alerts.

I had two missed messages which was unusual being as though no one ever leaves voicemails now a days. I turned on the water in the shower and pressed play. " You have two new unread messages. Say play to listen." The automated system said. "Play." I responded as I stepped into the shower allowing the water to caress my body. "You can't run!"

The same voice from the prank calls was now leaving me messages? I listened intensely since the audio was still recording but the voice was no longer speaking. It sounded like my buzzard. I stopped moving and put my ear closer to the phone to see if I could pick up anything. I jumped out of my skin when I heard myself on the voicemail saying hello. Whoever this was knew where I lived.

They rang the buzzer to my house and I responded to it. I had goosebumps. I took my wet index finger and swiped to the next message. I had to admit I was scared to even attempt to listen to the second message. "Hello, this is Michelle Hines. I am following up on a lead on a case involving El Fetche. Your name has come up a few times and I wanted to see if we could meet up. Please give me call back." If I was guilty of anything my heart would be sinking right now.

Since I know, not only do I not have anything to do with this – I can also send them looking into some deeper issues El Fetche may have an association with. I spent the rest of my time in the shower thinking and trying to understand who this mystery caller could be. It seems a tad bit odd that I began to get these calls today of all days. To be honest it could be Sonjay playing around, or it could be Nina being petty since she knows who I really am now. I turned on some jams just to get myself out my head. I needed a good vibe tonight. I wrapped up my shower still singing along to Erykah Badu.

She was always my go to if I needed a mellow aura about myself. It was like she spoke peace into the space. I took my time drying off. I was being super extra by grinding and making faces in the mirror. I laughed at myself realizing I was in good spirits. The music turned from cool smoker's vibe to a sensual Trey Songs atmosphere. I quickly turned off the music. I didn't want to set myself up for a long night of unpleasantries. As I brought the party of one to an end. I realized I wanted to dress semi casual.

I was in the comfort on my own home. I shouldn't have to be too formal for this meeting. I sent a quick text to India to see if things where still on for the evening. I had a little under an hour to prepare the meal. As of now everything was smooth sailing. I walked into the kitchen and placed a bottle of wine in the freezer. I lived for a chill glass. Just the thought of running out during dinner caused me to grab another bottle just in case.

I was pleased with myself. I had some fruit in the fridge and I decided make a quick basket just to set the mood. I played around a bit with the lighting in the room and I placed the files I needed for the evening beside my laptop. I jumped as the buzzer went off. This time I ran to the intercom. "Who is this?" I asked. At first there was no response. I repeated myself. This time I heard a familiar voice. "Hey I'm early I hope that's ok." It was India I didn't mind. It was better to be early than to be late.

I buzzed her in. I lit an incent to hide the strong marijuana smell. Moments later there was a tap at the door. I was still wearing my robe. I hope she wouldn't mind giving me more time to prepare. India was standing there holding her computer bag and a bottle of wine. I didn't want to overthink right off gate about her intentions. I am going to take the back seat right now and go from there. I welcomed her into my home super excited for the evening to start. I apologized for my attire and asked that she allow me a few minutes to get dressed. I was glad to see she wasn't super business. She looked normal, nothing spectacular.

So I made sure to dress down as well. I went as far as grabbing a few rompers to lounge around in. She was wearing shorts and a vest so I knew it wouldn't be a problem to wear my black romper with a nice maxi over top. I didn't bother putting on shoes. I slipped on a pair of socks. I checked myself in the mirror to make sure I was flawless. I walked out of the room feeling more confident. "Okayyyyy." I said as I re entered the room. "Well, I guess we should jump right in." I said as I joined India who was sitting on the couch watching the news. She smiled moving over a little to make room for me. I turned the lights up a tad. The mood was not there just yet.

Right now we needed to talk shop. She opened her computer bag and I began to prepare my items I wanted to present as well. Just as we were both settled the intercom buzzed. I excused myself and quickly responded to the intercom. "Delivery." A voice shouted. I buzzed them in. I asked my guest if she would like a glass of wine. I looked in the freezer and removed both bottles I placed in it earlier. She wanted a glass so I took down two regular sized wine glasses. I didn't want to scare her away to quick by taking a full bottle to the head. I handed her the glass and just in time there was a tap at the door.

I opened it and stepped back allowing the caterer to come in. I showed the crew where I needed them to set up. India joined me in the kitchen area being nosy. "Something smells divine." She said. "I would hope so. I hear they are the best in the city." I said embellishing a bit. I found them on a website hours ago. They continued to set up and we sheepishly watched them. I was ready for some good food. I felt India was authentic so I went with our roots. Her eyes were bulging as she watched the oxtails being stirred up. I grabbed her hand to lead her back to the couch. The crew had a job to do. Serve.

We also had things to discuss. I expected her to jerk away from me once my skin met hers but it didn't. In fact I tried to release her hand shortly after us turning around and she held onto my pinky finger. I didn't have her actual details on whether she like hotdogs or donuts. They say every straight girl wants that one gay friend that can service them whenever they want.

Under the right circumstances I might be willing to sign myself up for it. Things finally started flowing and we were starting to catch a good vibe. The news was still playing in the background but muted. The tunes was setting the a good rhythm in the house. According to India, she wanted to talk to me more about the business owner of El Fetche. She said a lot of big wigs had taken a huge hit in the last year or so and where all connected to El Fetche in one way or another.

I could tell she had done her homework in just a short time. The conversation was so good we completely forgot about dinner. We had a full spread presented before us and neither one of us paid any attention to it. We decided to take a break and enjoy our meal. I was prepared for India to say the grace like she did earlier. This time she drank and I dove right into my meal. The sauce on the oxtails was breathtaking. I was too busy digging in my plate to realize India still hasn't taken a bite to eat. I didn't care the food was spectacular. I took a moment to drink a little wine. India began to work up some rice and beans on her plate.

I secretly watched her take a bite. Her eyes closed and she had a food gasm. I smiled as I too understood what her taste buds where going through. We continued our conversation as we ate. I realized we could both do some damage in this city together. Time was passing by and I was feeling super accomplished. We had a good footing on what shall come out next on El Fetche. She has even convinced me to do a no face interview about a few topics. She asked for me to bring the receipts that prove what I am saying so she is not advertising lies.

I had no issue with accommodating her request. As the chef removed our plates and replaced them with a delightful slice of cheesecake, we held our glasses in the air and proposed a toast. India stood up and asked that I do the same. I took a bite out of my cheesecake before standing. Once I was on my feet. She asked the staff to wrap things up a little quicker and they obliged. I stood there looking at her like she was crazy.

She began to speak. "I wanted to say a few things to commemorate this evening." She said. I didn't respond, I allowed her to continue. It was obvious she was feeling her drink already. She swayed a little as she spoke. I thought it was cute. "Thank you for everything you are bringing to the table. I wanted to let you know sometimes in life we are presented with an opportunity. Some opportunities you know it is ok to bypass while others you know to take full advantage of it.

That's what we have here. An opportunity. So, thanks for that." India clanked her glass against mine and sat down. She began to fool around with her cheesecake. I was still standing wondering what she meant by opportunities. I didn't want to overthink it which I am certainly known for. I smiled and sat down slowly.

I took another bite out of my cheesecake. This time instead of tasting the creaminess It felt like I was chewing on rocks. I coughed a few times because it felt like I was choking. I looked down at my hand it was filled with blood, teeth and glass. I looked at India who didn't flinch. She wasn't trying to help me at all. I couldn't breathe. It felt like the more I coughed the more the shards of glass went down my throat. My vision was fading but I was able to see one face clearly as I fell to my death. It was Jodi. She got me.

Chapter 10- Nina-

Loose Ends I sat in the bed flicking through Netflix thinking of all the times Tae and I shared. She was more than a friend. She was my sister, backbone and voice of reason. It was a lot going on around me but nothing was more important than Tae. I wanted business to get back up and running but we must go through a remodel on one side of the building. Me personally, I would rather leave and purchase a new office space. Rico said it wasn't good to dip out and rebuild. I figured it would be ok once the insurance money came through. It is all depending on what they find as the source of the incident.

I can't catch a break but at the same time I know I am doing the best I can. I had a lot of moving parts I needed to sort through. Roe was able to get me home which I am super grateful, but she had to leave in a hurry. I hadn't heard anything else from her once she dipped out. Rico and I spent time together. He held me until I didn't want to be held anymore. I thanked him so much for that. He still had a lot of things to explain about his whereabouts over the past few days. I had written things off due to the circumstances, but it is time for him to provide me with something.

I received a text from Jodi sending her condolences. I didn't respond back right away but the next day I did. I asked her why. That's all I could say was why. She didn't take long before she was wanting to check in on me and started calling the job every hour. I get it. She might have a little thing for me, but Rico is not going to have that. At least not while he is around. He doesn't have a problem with the sexuality aspect. However, he would have high expectations that we wouldn't make it a week without him ending her life. I smiled at the thought of him going up against someone so small. I had to check him at the hospital a few days ago because he did something to Jodi. I heard a lot of commotion in the room next to me.

It sounded like pain and agony. I can only hope he didn't harm her too bad. I had no other choice but to mind my business and lay low. Problem was Rico can get a bit out of hand at times and it is hard to control him and his Cubans. I wanted more for his life. It was nice having him back around and I know people still give me the side eye for even talking to him after the stunts he has pulled. I honestly think all that anger went away when Felecia and Mr. X died last year.

I thought everything would be behind us and then I find out Jess is Jasmyn. Jodi was involved somehow but I don't know how. Sonjay was another issue within itself. Sometimes dealing with high profile clients can be challenging. He really put us in jeopardy. I felt horrible for Roe and Tati. They had to deal with his madness because he is family.

I always wondered if the men who indulged in my company act the same way around their wives or mates and spouses. Why be someone different but how can I complain when I have built an industry that allows you to embrace your differences. My heart still broke for Tae, Tyesha and Kyle. Kyle was a dickhead manipulated by Sonjay but otherwise he seemed like an ok guy. I didn't know him but he was way more apologetic than Sonjay was. I had to give him points for that.

What I didn't understand was why would Jas or should I say Jess want to go after Kyle instead of Sonjay? He would have been the bigger target in my eyes. My brain was starting to hurt from over processing. I would do that sometimes when I was overly stressed. I was the kind of person who had to make perfect sense out of everything. As I get older I see now it doesn't matter if you don't want to play the game. You are the game. Period. At any moment anyone can take me down. I am hoping I am surrounded by enough people who would never let that happen. You never know sometimes. Funny thing about having power is nothing happens in your territory without me finding out about it. I heard through the grapevine I had a few people who were willing to share a few stories about me for a few coins. At first I was bothered.

Then I thought, how can we turn those rotten lemons into lemonade? Why not allow them to expose El Fetche. What I have learned over the time I have been in business, is; sometimes you must allow a good casual debate about healthy fetishes and people are afraid to say out loud. Just the thought of it makes me want to turn my own self in. Times are changing and things are not the normal missionary society it used to be. Now we are dealing with new millennium people. They are down with trying new things and making new memories. Sometimes you must let things play out on their own and I was certainly willing to allow the stories to hit the scene.

I knew Roe would make sure I was ok in the event something happens. I told myself last year, I wasn't going to be a coward. I was not going to run away from my issues. I was adult enough to admit when I was wrong but I was also human and didn't like to be wrong. I didn't do anything and I had nothing to do with the fire. They only thing I should be guilty of was forcing everyone in a room to discuss a matter in which could have ruined everyone involved. How can I be blamed for that.

I even had a resolution prior to leaving the meeting. My thoughts were beginning to unravel all over again. I was startled when I heard my phone vibrating. I hadn't been taking any calls but the same number continued to call me. This time I decided to answer. "Yeah?" I said with frustration. "Hey. It's me. Jodi." I heard a faint voice say on the other end. "Jodi?" I said trying to figure out why she was on my phone. "Before you hang up just please… hear me out for 1 second." She was practically begging me to talk to her. I wasn't mad about her situation with Jess or Jas- whatever she likes to be called. I was disappointed in her because I saw something in her.

She had become apart of our little situation at work. I told her to make it quick. "Listen, If I make things right can I please have my job back. I had to admit I was seen toting cameras and audio clips and even drugs inside the rooms. I didn't know what it was for but I did as I was told At the time it was brought to me as if I was installing for security measures. I had no idea this footage would leak back and be on something super bogus. I also need you to understand that Jasmyn doesn't look like she used to. She did something with her face and it threw me off. I won't front. It threw me all the way off. I need to fix this. Please let me."

She asked. I held out my hand and looked over my newly polished nails. I didn't know what to say. I would generally leave things like this up to Tae. I took a deep breath before responding. When it was time for me to say something. I came up speechless. This was a little unusual but seriously. What is it that I needed to say. It sounded like a bunch of bad coincidences. Then again could it be more. I had more questions but didn't want to cloud my mind with another unsolved mystery.

"It depends on what you bringing to the table. Don't hit me until you got something good. It's either that or simply deal with Rico from this point on." My voice was strictly on monotone. I really didn't care what she had up her sleeve as long as it didn't circle back to me I was good with it. Before letting her go I told her it was good to hear she was still breathing.

Last time I caught a glimpse of her was when she ran into Rico at the hospital. I was just about to be questioned and he saw her in the room next door. As I said earlier, in my line of business there is always so many moving parts. We ended our call and I sat there for a moment thinking exactly what do she think she can do to get back in my good graces. I let it roll in one ear and out the other. I didn't want to wonder about everyone else. I wanted to run away. I needed to smoke. It was the only thing I could think of to get my mind off things.

Of course we all have our problems but geesh.. can I have a smooth twenty-four months without any drama? Just as I was getting filled with anxiety, Rico walked into the room. I didn't even know he was here. This house was entirely too big hence the reason I like to stay at my property in the city. "Hey beautiful." He said as he walked through the bedroom door bringing nothing but sunshine with him. His smile was heavenly. His eyes were troubled. "What's going on?"

I asked. I didn't allow my internal excitement to show. "We got to talk." He said. I hated when he started our conversations like this. He was the awkward guy who says that and then will break out some good news. You never know what you're going to get. I sat at the edge of the bed waiting on him to say whatever he needed to. Seemed like everyone was in the mood to talk to me. "Sonjay hasn't been out of his house.

Last time I saw him, Roe was leaving the house. I am not sure what happened from that point but there has been no movement in his house since." Rico looked over at me as if I would have some profound solution for him. I returned his look and pressed my lips together. "So what?" I asked. The more he sat there the more frustrated I got. "We need our check." He said. "Then get it."

I said as I finally stood to my feet and pushed past him. Seriously what did he want me to do about it. He was the muscle of this operation. If he was so concerned about his check, he would have collected the money before anyone even left. I couldn't deal with him right now. I couldn't deal with anyone at this point. I hit Roe up to see what she was doing. I should have taken her up on her offer and went back to the city with her. I also wanted to catch up with her and see if her sister was ok. I couldn't imagine being in that situation and not having an outlet.

Sonjay was more than a dog he was a dirty dog with flees. It was ridiculous to say the least. I do feel he should be held accountable for the murder of that girl. I couldn't fathom the thought of sleeping with a man capable of raping a woman. I was already on a thin line sleeping with a man who could crush a life with one blow. I had to admit, I liked having a sense of danger close by. It was like adding a little spice in my life.

I grabbed my keys and decided to take a ride. Before I could walk out the door Rico grabbed my wrist. "I wasn't done." He said. I looked at him like he was crazy. I wanted to make sure I gave him the time he needed but I also needed to simply clear my mind. "I sent a crew into his house earlier this morning. I haven't heard anything back yet." He held his head down and a look of defeat came across his face. "I hate when I have to get dirty Nina." He said. He really wanted to do and be better in life. Being involved with all my drama has him out of his comfort zone.

I thought all this mess was over but its clear another dollar another dead body. I walked over to him and kissed him gently. I whispered in his ear to control the controllable. There is nothing we could do to fix any of this at this point. I don't intend on waving my white flag. Just as he was about to respond his phone went off. I caught a glimpse of the name. It was Jodi. I looked at him super weird.

They hated each other so why was she calling him? I didn't raise any alarm I knew when to say something and when not to. I walked away heading out the door per my original plan. Rico tried to grab me once more but this time

I slipped out of his hands. I was ready for the air. Roe finally hit me back inviting me over. I was so glad she responded. I knew if I talked to someone it needed to be her. She was legally bound to listen to me without judgement. She was unable to release what I tell her due to client privilege. She sent me a pin address via text and as soon as I hopped in one of the trucks in the drive way, I lit my joint and headed back to the city.

I was emotionally exhausted and I wanted to sort things out. I needed to make sense of things. I began to take things from the top. Prior to this case, things were good. Tae began to build her girls up more clientele. It began to flood over into a whole international movement. She was starting to get women from everywhere. They were legit though.

They came with real visas. Reality was we didn't know that money meant anything until it was spent internationally. We were talking about opening an actual location there. I was entertaining the idea of leaving the country. Jas (Jess)was one of our heavy hitters to be honest. She had clients who would specifically ask for her. If she was not available they would pass. Tears began to roll down my eyes as I thought of how Tae gave Jas a chance. Jodi said something that made sense to me. She looked different. I feel like that wasn't the first time I heard that. It's a little extreme.

Maybe even farfetched. I guess I want to know who goes through all that mess to get revenge. Especially revenge that was never yours to seek anyways. Its foolish. It dawned on me that things were not as clear as I thought. I remember there was another chick we employed who loved being booked with Jas. I had no say so over the girls plans for the most part that was all Tae. I should have known something was fishy.

Things were simply going too well. My mind drifted to Tyesha and Kyle. That poor girl. She had the balls bigger than a horse to take on this challenge.

According to Roe, her sister Tati and Tyesha were best friends from childhood. She said they all were close. Imagine that, you and your best friend just so happen to be married to raping murderers. Like whoa. The amount of aggression it takes to brutally rape someone to the point where they are no longer breathing is sickening. What made it worse was the friends were sticking together to find out the truth of this case.

Once the meeting happened that gut feeling I had walking into the vault let me know I was right. Lives would change. There was no other way around it. That night a lot of dirty secrets were dropped like bombs over Baghdad. Roe mentioned things where heating up when she left the room between Kyle and Ty. I couldn't say I didn't expect that to happen. Lets be honest. Could you sit in the same room as your husband and watch a sex tape of him exposing himself to everyone in the room?

It was embarrassing to say the least. If I was a fly on the wall. I couldn't wrap my mind around why Tae was still in the room. Her body was right at the door. Why not open it. Was the door trapped from the outside? I began to get enraged thinking of what her last moments must have been like. I wanted Kyle to pay for this but he was no longer here to blame.

The only person left is Sonjay who apparently has gone missing. I didn't get the entire story so who knows how things will end. I can only imagine Sonjay did something extravagant by leaving the country to avoid paying out his debts. I continued smoking and letting the wind blow in my hair. I needed this. I wanted this freedom feeling. It was the perfect timing.

My emotions were uncontrollable. I was so tired of feeling like I was on the brink of losing everything. I can't share my inner me with anyone because its clear they only like me when I am pretending to be someone else. I was Nina Toussaint. I was no chump. The smoke was getting so good I hadn't realized there was a car behind me. I wasn't alarmed just making note of a vehicle. I put my joint out in the ashtray and turned down my radio.

I am not sure why black people associate loud music with being a good driver. It was apart of our "let me sober up real quick" routine. I laughed thinking of the many conversations Tae and I shared on the road. There were multiple times where things got real and we had to sober up real quick. The car behind me must be in a hurry they were starting to ride my tail a little. I looked down and realized I was going under the speed limit. I couldn't do anything but break out in major laughter.

I laughed so hard I cried as I did my best to speed up a little. I was high, my reaction to things were a little delayed. They would simply have to bare with me while I get myself together. The second lane finally opened and within seconds the car behind me sped past me. I wasn't mad. I couldn't say anything. To be honest I was wrong and if I wasn't high I would have been upset if it was happening to me. I didn't care. I felt helpless. I still haven't sped up enough to keep up with traffic and I just didn't feel like I had the intentions to do so. Thank goodness the GPS was chiming for me to take the next exit. I finally made it in the city.

I decided to ride past the office on my way to Roe's. It didn't take long before I saw the reflection of failure flash before my eyes. I hated when the enemy wins. I didn't want to shut my business down but I do believe I need to relocate. Life has been sending me direct messages that I am obviously missing. What did I do that put such a curse on my life. I don't display my actual thoughts and feelings to many especially people around me. I needed Tae so bad. I decided to turn the truck around and park in the deck. I sat there for a moment debating on going inside. I said screw it and turned off the truck and headed into the building. There was yellow tape everywhere.

I did my best to be careful as I stepped on broken glass and debris. I slowly made my way towards the situation vault. I just needed to see things from my own perspective. I turned the lights on in the building but the situation vault still was without electricity. I walked over to my office and grabbed a flashlight. I walked into the vault. It was a mess in there. Ventilation was hanging from the ceiling, dry wall had burned down exposing the steel in the room. There where white outlines where bodies where found. I held the bottom of my shirt up to my nose.

It was clear I needed to protect myself from inhaling the soot left in the room. I continued to walk through the room. When I noticed something sitting on the table in the corner. It was flashing red. It was small. I couldn't tell what it was and to be honest I was scared it could have been me coming face to face with a creature of the night. I took the flash light and shinned it around the room just to make sure I was still alone.

I was creeped out. Lets be honest three peoples souls at least could still be trapped in here. I finally reached the table. I started fumbling around until I found the little red light. It was a phone. It was an iPhone. It was going dead and the back of the phone looked a tad distorted. It was covered up by a half broken lamp shade. I didn't allow phones to be used in this room.

So who would have kept their phone on the table? I wondered if I could try to use the phone. I placed it in my pocket and made my way out of the vault. I was super intrigued. I wanted to charge the phone so bad to see if we could possibly get anything off of it. I wanted to show Roe what I had found so I needed to wrap things up. Before leaving the building I said a small prayer and opened the doors allowing any trapped spirits to be released. I didn't know for sure what I planned to do with the building, but for right now, I needed to grieve. I needed a break from it all. I remember feeling the same way before. I don't want to continue to relive the same experiences. Its time for something else. Before I let it go, I did plan to go out with a bang in more ways than one.

As I hopped back in the truck my phone got an alert. It was a voicemail. Someone must have called when I went inside the building. I figured I would check the voicemail later. I had to get to Roe's house. I was right up the street from what it looked like. Within a few minutes I was texting Roe letting her know I was outside. She had done nice for herself. I guess being a lawyer paid off.

I waited for the door to open prior to me exiting the vehicle. I had seen enough horror movies of the black girl getting out the car and someone sneaks up on her from behind. It looked like the prefect neighborhood for a good scandal. I grabbed my bags and walked to the door quickly. It was a young man who greeted me. He was handsome. He introduced himself as MJ.

I responded by embracing him. I needed a pure hug and it was the perfect opportunity to get it. He smiled and embraced me back. He grabbed my bag and said his mother had a bed made up for me. I was getting the royal treatment in which I oh so deserved. I reached for my phone and turned down the volume. I didn't want to be disturbed. Rico could handle things on his end hopefully.

Right now, I just wanted to focus on the most important person. Myself. I reached the top of the staircase and MJ showed me to the east wing of the property. Roe made sure I had an entire section to myself. I thank goodness I met her in Bora Bora. Who knew we would be here? This entire experience is humbling. Each year brings a bigger challenge but guess what? They can't stop me. I reached the master bedroom and MJ dropped my bag on the floor. "Buzz us if you need anything Mrs. Toussaint." MJ said as he excused himself. He was such a gentleman.

I was impressed. It was like he was more than a gentleman; he was trained. I couldn't put my finger on it but a young man such as him should be a tad more loose. I didn't let his social awkwardness bother me. I wanted to see Roe. I did just as MJ instructed. I gave his mom a buzz. I walked around the room waiting on her to respond back. It didn't take long before her voice came exulting out of the intercom. "Ninaaaaa. I am glad you made it. I figured you wanted to have some time alone but I'm on the other side of the house if you need anything.

"She said without taking a breath. She was excited it seems. "Thanks for having me. I think I should be ok for the night, but I am starving. Please tell me something delivers out here." I asked. Just being in this space was giving me life. The room was spacious. I was surrounded by pure white linen everywhere. I took my shoes and jeans off because I didn't want to get anything dirty. It was breathtaking.

I hadn't went into the bathroom yet but I was sure it would be nothing but perfection. "Ahhhh… Sure I think so. I say try it but if not feel free to find something to eat downstairs." She responded. I took her advice and started to look through apps to see who would deliver. I kicked back on the bed for a moment and turned the tv on. I didn't want to stroll through the channels just yet. I needed to find something to fill my belly with. As usual I was side tracked when the voicemail icon popped up once more on my screen.

I decided since I was in a safe place I could press play. "Message # 1 – Hey Nina, -It's me. Jodi. I've got something to tell you. It's all over. I will call you soon." I didn't want to know what she had done. I knew it was something I wouldn't want any part of. However I had to admit I was intrigued. I wanted to call her back but the tone of her voice sounded like she might need to lay low for a while. Message 2 Nina- ok.

We need to talk. This is the detective down at the Buckhead County Sherriff office. Now I have given you time to gather yourself. I think its about time we had ourselves another conversation. The phone fumbled a bit and his voice trailed off. I could hear someone in the background. It sounded like a woman.

She was begging him to hang up. I couldn't really tell if It was a struggle or if she wanted his attention on personal level. I replayed the message to see if I could possibly catch the voice on it. I was completely side tracked at this point. I was starving but I was also feeling like a private detective. Its almost like I was given a new nose and I could smell for the first time. I tried to shake off the new smells but it was like they were calling me. I had to dig deeper. I dialed Mr. Watson back. I was up on my feet pacing back and forth until he answered.

Moments later- I got his voicemail. I decided to leave him a message. I cleared my throat just as the beep noise went off to record. "This is Nina Toussaint, returning a phone call to Detective Watson. I am finally getting settled for the evening but would be delighted to speak with you sometime tomorrow. I look forward to hearing from you with a good time." I hung up the phone and played his voicemail once more.

Something wasn't right. Why would someone tell him to hang up the phone. I didn't want to turn into a mad women so I got back to the original task at hand. Food. I was still starving and I could feel my blood sugar starting to get low. I scrolled through a few spots when I decided to order something quick and easy. I selected a delivery for pizza. I knew it would be good and hot once it got here.

I had a few minutes until my delivery so I took the time to look for a charger that could fit the phone I found. I was scared to try and charge it to be honest. What if it still has water on the inside of it. Can I get shocked? I sent a quick text to Roe asking her to come join me. I told her to bring something to drink, a bag of chips and different charging cords.

She laughed but not once did she question it. She was giving me the perfect amount of support I feel like I need right now. Just as she arrived into the room the tv began to give us an update. I was holding my breath hoping it was nothing else dealing with El Fetche. That would send me over the edge. As the news reporter begins her story I realized they where not in front of my building so I was ok with it.

The headline read: Dinner and Death. I had to admit I was relieved but also totally here for the headline. Roe laughed as she noticed I was preparing to have myself a good evening. "Can I smoke in here?" I asked. "Depends on what you're smoking." She replied We giggled a little and I reached for a fresh joint out of my bag. She looked over at me and pulled a lighter out of her boob. "Here chile. Light that." Roe said and I did just as she asked.

We continued to watch tv. We were waiting until they gave more details on the report about dinner and death. We heard a buzz coming from the intercom. It was MJ letting me know my pizza was here. I told him he could have some and he needs to bring the rest up to us. He complied. It didn't take long before he was running up the steps. He was out of breath by the time he made it up the steps.

I laughed because it felt good to see someone else struggle with those steps the same way I did. "Mama- Tati is sitting outside in her car." Said MJ bringing it to Roe's attention. Her sister was sitting in the driveway this late at night. Roe wore a look of confusion on her face.

She grabbed her phone and called her sister. No answer. She was starting to make me worry. I asked that she be careful. She brushed me off and said no need to worry.

She would be back in a few minutes. MJ and I enjoyed our pizza. I didn't want him in the room to be honest because I wanted to keep smoking but I was in someone else house so I wanted to behave. It wasn't like he was going to mind anyways. He was a sweet boy but you can tell he is a little off. He might need to hit this joint to get his mind right. I won't pass it to him though that's for his mama to do.

MJ grabbed the remote and started flickering through the channels. I didn't mind. I was too busy on my own phone. I wasn't a big social media person but I dabbled a bit in making an app for El Fetche. It was to bring in our younger millionaires. The only thing I don't like about it would be a mandatory response being required for the new member to see people who may want to link up. It was like that popular site Face tag or something like that.

All new members get that welcome message from the founder. Instead of having that on an automatic setting I had it set to where after a certain amount of new accounts created I will welcome them as a group. As time went passed we noticed Roe hadn't returned. It had been at least thirty minutes since she went to check on Tati. MJ had dozed off on the bed. Surprisingly I didn't mind. I was never the one for children but I didn't mind it at all. He was laying there so peacefully with his legs folded up to his chest. I didn't want to wake him so I eased my way to the edge of the bed and slid off of it.

My feet hit plush carpet and I looked for some slides in my overnight bag. I checked my phone once more before leaving MJ fast asleep. As I got closer to the steps I could hear voices. The closer I go to the bottom the louder the voices echoed. I reached the bottom of the steps I tipped toed towards the kitchen. I didn't want to interrupt them by making a lot of noise. It was obvious it was a very intense conversation.

As I got closer I figured out what the argument was over. Sonjay. Things may look good around here but they are on a total different level of bad. I saw Roe sitting at the kitchen bar with her sister Tati. Roe was holding her hand trying to console her over him. Tati's entire demeanor seemed…off. I decided to interject myself. Being as though Sonjay is no where to be found, maybe it was good idea to get the full scoop.

I walked in the kitchen humming as if I wasn't just standing there drinking up the gossip. "Excuse me ladies. Hey Tati. How are you?" I asked. I was still holding my joint so I sparked it in the kitchen. Roe looked relieved to see me so I kept the same energy. I opened the fridge and saw a bottle of Jack Daniels waiting on me. I grabbed it and asked for a glass and Roe got up from the bar to hand me on.

"Nina?" What are you doing here? Well…. Actually no. I'm sorry. I should be asking how are you doing and feeling." Tati greeted me but she was still off. I continued to poke the bear a little to feel her out. "So how are things for you. I am so sorry about your loss." I said trying to let her know it was a safe space. "Same to you Nina. Losing our best friends so suddenly can be a lot to process. But, I am here." She said as she pushed an empty glass towards me. She wanted a drink as well. I obliged. Roe joined in and pushed a glass up for herself. I asked them both if I was interrupting and neither responded.

The room was tense. We sat in silence for at least two minutes sitting and breathing over our glasses. I passed the joint to Tati. She took it and inhaled deep. Roe was just as shocked as I was. I didn't say anything because it was clear she was wearing the weight of the world on her shoulders. "How's your husband?" I asked trying to break the ice. Roe eyes got big as if she didn't want to hear the answer to the question. My attention was all over this situation. These ladies needed to spill the beans. Roe began to answer but Tati cut her off. "As his wife , I would say he was home in bed tucked in preparing for a long day of work in the morning. Roe, since you're his baby's mama how would you say my husband is?" Tati said just as calmly as she wants to be. She turned and faced Roe allowing her to take the floor. "Tati. Come on.

We can be adults about this right?" She asked. I didn't move a muscle. Roe business was on the table. I just ate pizza but whatever they serving I am here for it. I removed myself from the bar and slid over to the actual dinning table. I was still smoking and I was sure MJ was still sleeping. We were going to have us a nice vibe in here tonight. I refilled my drink. And took a sip.

Roe was pleading her case on how things got started and was begging for forgiveness. Tati on the other hand was riled up. She walked over to the bottle of Jack Daniels and instead of refilling her glass she grabbed it and took it to the head. "What makes you think I care? No matter the circumstances you was wrong Roe. Its cool though. I came to get some things off my chest." Tati began shouting with every word she said. I wanted to hop in there but this was something that would just have to play out.

I tried to be the voice of reasoning. I didn't have a sister. Tae was the closest thing to a sister. They needed to make up. I tapped my nails on the table bringing the room to a halt. "I understand this is frustrating. However it takes two to tango. Where is Sonjay and what has he said about this all?" I asked. Now that it released from my lips I am not sure if it was really a devils advocate situation.

Maybe it was more of a -I'm nosey and I need more details. It felt good to sip on someone else's tea for a chance. I was exhausted and totally fed up with the amount of drama in my world. Tati looked at me before responding. Her eyes turned cold and the energy shifted in the room.

"He can't say anything. When he was able to say something, I honestly didn't like the bs he was feeding me." Tati started smiling. It was sinister. Roe and I connected eyes and both displayed a frantic look. Tati was still holding the bottle of Jack and had taken the last sip. The bottle was full when I poured my first glass. I really didn't know what to say.

  The only thing I could think of is ways to leave this space unharmed. My gun was in my bag upstairs and I also left my phone up there. I slowly looked down as Tati was still ranting about her deceased husband. I was relieved to see I was wearing my smart watch. The house was so big I didn't know if it would be able to pull a signal. I was pissed to be honest. A dead man can't pay debts. I knew once I tell Rico he would be going after Tati for money. My joint was starting to burn out but it was the perfect opportunity to get up and make sure it is no longer lit.

  I stood slowly and Tati didn't budge. Her energy was for Roe more so than me. I walked over to the sink, I quickly sent a pin location to whoever sent me a message to my phone last. I hope it was someone who had some sense. I didn't want to scroll through my watch making any unwarranted movement. Tati was pacing. Seemed like her anger was starting to subside. Which was always good. I had my ear to her mouth for the most part of her rant. She was in a dark place and some of the things she was saying has me confused as to who Roe really is. Her son had to be at least just hitting puberty.

  Has she been checking for Sonjay this entire time? How could someone that close to you sleep with your man numerously. Apparently before Sonjay was murdered, he let Tati know things he had done to other women. Roe was his side chick for the same amount of time he was with her sister. How much evil do you have to embody to pull off something so vile. As I continued to listen to her try to plead her case, she didn't have one.

Roe was flat out wrong. Tati's pacing sped up and started to become more sporadic. Roe was just like Jas and Felecia. She was someone who made moves based upon the hard work and labor of others. I never thought I could see her like that. She wasn't like that in Bora Bora. Tae and I explained to them what we had just overcome. We laid it out on the table that we wanted to have a new bond with a group of women who could empower and uplift. I felt we were doing that.

Instead Roe was sneaking around just like the deadbeats. I was shocked. I was disgusted. Tati was now sitting by Roe who was no longer pleading her case. I was standing in front of the sink frozen. I didn't know for sure if my ping went out for my location. I knew even though I felt where Tati was coming from, that was her sister and her nephew is upstairs. I walked around the massive counter. I didn't move too fast. Once I was on the same side as them both I noticed Tati was holding something. It was poking Roe in the rib cage.

You could see how uncomfortable she was with it being lodged in her side. I approached her letting her know I was not going to harm her. I just wanted to take the gun. Tati pushed the gun into Roe's side a little more. "Why care about her. She didn't care about me." Tati cried. She was hurt. She had every right to be. "You think she loyal to you? I'm sure she has tried to sleep with your man too honey so you better go fact check that.!!"

She was throwing out all kind of shots now. I was letting them roll off my back. Rico should know better but tonight was not about him. I finally reached them both. I reached my arm out and began to grab for the gun. Just as I was about to have control MJ yelled down to check on us. He sounded concerned. He scared us all causing us to tussle over the gun.

Finally one single shot let out. We all stopped in our tracks. The house fell quiet. We all looked around at each another and there was no blood on us. We took deep breaths and let out an easy sigh. Moments later we heard a loud thud. We all scurried towards the noise to see what it was. Before we could make it around the corner. There was a pool of blood covering the tile floor in the foyer. MJ's body was distorted. He had fallen down the steps, after a bullet hit him. It was so much blood we couldn't see what needed to be done to make him ok. His eyes had nothing left to say.

Both Roe and Tati where screaming at the top of their lungs. Roe was on her knees trying to get the blood to stop. Tati was literally pulling her hair out. Things where totally getting out of control. I had to snap into full Nina mode. "Hey! Hey!" I shouted. "Calm down. Tears are not going to get this under control." I said. I was pissed on the low. Tati had placed me in a situation that I wanted nothing to do with. The murder of a kid. Like how was I going to explain this? I started shouting demands, I sent Tati upstairs to grab my phone.

I sent Roe to get some cleaning products. It didn't take long before Tati was back down stairs holding my phone so tight the screen began to change colors. I gave her more instructions. I had to keep her moving. There was no way I could let them sit and sulk. We could do that later. She joined Roe cleaning up the blood and I began to lay large black trash bags under MJ. I wanted to be able to remove him easily from the steps. I knew I would have to do it alone. There was no way either of them could help with this part.

I took my phone out quickly snapping a picture. It was always good to have proof of things. I looked to see who I sent the address to earlier. I was totally disappointed to see it was Jodi. She didn't respond back thank goodness so I immediately called Rico. The phone didn't ring long before he was answering."Nin…" He answered. "Come to me. Bring the clean up crew." I said and disconnected the call. I sent him the address and I knew he would be here soon. I had to keep moving until he came. Roe was on her hands and knees wiping up traces of blood. MJ's body remained lifeless just two steps before his mothers head. I asked her to move for a second and I did my best to be gentle and move his body.

I asked her to walk away to another room for a few minutes. She complied. Tati stood at the bottom of the steps beside me. She wanted to help me. We used a large industrial bag and shoved him into it. My heart was breaking for him. Just as I was making sure the bag was closed the front door flew open. Tati and I were both startled. It was Jodi. She had come to my rescue. I had to admit I was a little impressed. Maybe she was still wanting to prove her loyalty. This was the best time to do it. Her eyes grew big as she saw Tati and I toting the bag. She immediately closed the door and took off her shoes. "What happened here?"

She asked as she walked over to my side of the bag and moved me out of her way. She took over and I decided to help Roe in the other room. Tati and Jodi moved the body to another space downstairs. I grabbed Roe's hand and led her to the kitchen table. She sat down, still unable to speak. She only had pain behind her eyes. They were blood red. She was breathing heavy and her leg was shaking. I reached my hand over and grabbed hers. She made eye contact with me.

I noticed she had a few spots of blood on her face. I couldn't let her sit here like this. I grabbed her and helped her stand up. I needed to take her upstairs to clean her up along with laying her down until we figure out what to do. We took the small elevator for servers. I didn't want her to walk past the steps right now. Once we arrived, she showed me how to get to her room.

We stumbled a bit but we made it to the master bathroom. She hadn't stopped crying. I was worried she was going to be dehydrated with the amount of tears she was leaking. I ran some bath water for her and I sat her down on the vanity seat. She faced her mirror and broke down even more. She was asking me why this has happened to her baby and I didn't want to tell her that karma don't have a name on it.

Unfortunately, MJ paid for the sins of his parents. This entire evening was a wreck. I could hear commotion downstairs. It sounded like a vacuum or some sorts. I grabbed a wash cloth and turned on the faucet. There was a bar of soap sitting on the sink. I took it and lathered up her wash cloth. I told her to wash her face for me while I checked on things down stairs. I turned off the bath water. I didn't want it to overflow.

Roe agreed to get herself together. I went back downstairs to see what was going on. Once I was down I noticed the cleaning crew was here. Tati was sitting in the living room and there was a group of six cleaning up the space. Jodi was sitting at the kitchen bar with Rico. It was a sight for sore eyes but they were having a discussion. It wasn't the kind of discussion that would lead to any blows. This time it looked to be more of a civilized conversation that could potentially end with a fist pound. " Thanks yall for showing up." I said.

Things were starting to look back to normal. Well as normal as can be. Both said I was welcome. Rico said it was a good time to bury a few things. He had a proposition for me. He wanted me to bring Jodi back into security. This time he would like to be her direct boss. I was confused. I didn't expect for these fools to become the best of friends. "Jodi must have done something major to be considered as an employee again." I said.

She was only here tonight by default. They both looked at me as if I was speaking a foreign language. I pulled up a chair right between the both of them. I needed them to help me see their vision. In a world full of chaos these fools are back here harmonizing with one another. "Let's hear it." I said. Rico took the floor. Look we not going to draw this out. We made a truths and it is clear she wants to hold you down just as much as I do." Rico was serious. He was looking at me without blinking. I felt he meant what he was saying.

"I asked you if there was something I could do to make things right. Well. I did something that will work out for the better for all parties involved." She stopped talking. I didn't poke or ask questions. I think we all knew this space wasn't for that kind of conversation. There was enough going on around us. We sat there in silence. I wasn't ready to make any decisions. I would put it in the parking lot for later.

Right now we needed to get the cleaning crew out of here before the sun comes up. I got up from the table and went to join Tati. She was now laying on the sofa in a fetal position. Tonight must be a mental overload. She was laying in a puddle of tears. No one would have known a tragedy had taken place here. The hard part will be the aftermath. How do you explain a kid who was just in China exploring the world. I was drained. I know everything happens for a reason. I can't find the reason yet but we will some way. I shook Tati a bit and told her to get up and join Roe in bed. I needed to go back up and check on her. I knew I was not going to stay here for the night. It was just way too much happening.

The clean up crew exited the home just as quiet as they had crept in. She was still shaking. The adrenaline must be starting to wear off. I treated her just as gentle as I did Roe. It was a lot of hurt between the two of them and I can only imagine this has pushed them over the edge. When the liquor is no longer swimming around in their system things will get weird. It didn't take long for me to get Tati down and tucked in. I joined Rico and Jodi downstairs. I was holding my bags in my hand. I collected my things while I was upstairs. I sat back down taking a deep breath. I was exhausted. I dropped my bags on the ground and reached for my phone. I was getting a call from Detective Watson.

The sun was literally starting to come up. The entire point of me coming here was for peace. I looked around and realized my chaos was my peace. I ignored his call. My thoughts were interrupted when Rico asked if I heard anything from Sonjay. He asked me the same thing earlier. This time I was able to give some feedback. I told him Tati took care of him. He disagreed. He said his men went in and no one was there. It was plenty of blood there but no signs of a body. I was completely thrown off.

Tati never mentioned how she got rid of his body. Something wasn't sitting right with me. If she didn't kill him, where is he? Before I could verbally process what I was intending to work out in my head, Rico's head was being smashed against the bar counter top. Jodi and I both jumped and screamed confused as to what was going on. I turned to look and see who was responsible for this and it was him. Sonjay.

He wasn't dead. His shirt was bloody as if he had been in a heated fight. Where did he come from? Jodi warned me to duck as he was trying to swing at my head. I did as she told me and dropped to the floor. I crawled around the other side and began looking in the drawers for a knife. Jodi sounded like she was getting the beating of her life. I grabbed my phone and dialed Detective Watson's number.

I didn't have time to talk to him so I slid the phone on the counter. Just as soon as I stood up Sonjay was across the room choking Jodi. Jodi was struggling to grab the vase beside her. I decided to play target practice. I began to unload every knife in the drawer. I stuck a few in his back from across the room. I had to admit I had good aim. Rico was bleeding out on the counter. There was no way he could be alive. Jodi had fallen to her knees and Sonjay was trying to get the knives out of his back. He backed into a chair causing one of the knives to go deeper into his back. He screamed out in pain. Jodi found the metal bat he was once using on Rico and hit him multiple times bringing him to his knees. Jodi looked over just in time to warm me Tati had gotten off the elevator.

"Don't MOVE!" She shouted. "All of you have ruined my life." She was holding another gun. She was packing tonight because it wasn't the same gun we wrestled with earlier. I dropped the remaining weapons I was holding and held my hands up. "Seriously Tati?" I said. "All of this?" You're risking your entire world over a broken heart? "I was trying to say anything to keep her from pulling that trigger. "Maybe not all of this. It worked out well. MJ just so happen to be a casualty but the death of everyone else is on the menu. How dare you tell my man what he will pay for in a case. If he said he didn't do anything then I believe him.

You all are sick. I can't wait to end this." She shouted. Sonjay was slowly trying to adjust himself. Blood was gushing from his mouth. He was dying. Jodi was slowly making her way over to me step by step. Sonjay started coughing causing Tati to be concerned. "Come on baby. Don't die on me. Please." She begged. Her hands were shaking repulsively. I noticed Jodi looking towards the window. I couldn't turn around to see what she was seeing but I just remained calm and tried to talk Tati down. "Tati, where is Roe? Is she still sleeping?" I asked. "Nope. Killed her too.

You think I am playing with all yall freaks?" You can't play with people heart and get away with it. So now is the time for you to make peace with your maker." She said. Her gun didn't have one in the chamber. I heard her click it into place. I took advantage and ducked once more just as her hand was releasing the trigger. Gun shots began to ring out from everywhere. Tati's body ricocheted from the hits. Jodi has come to the ground with me. The sound of glass shattering and aggressive commands being yelled at us asking us to stay down. My heart was beating hard. Officers in black suits came and patted me down.

They placed zip ties on my hands and feet and drug me out the door to the grassy area. My head was hurting so bad, but I looked over and saw Jodi tied up just as I was. They had us both. Everything took a drastic turn. Minutes later Detective Watson was helping me off the ground. He cut the restraints and asked me if I was ok. He did the same for Jodi. Once she was sitting up she joined me. We both had been through a traumatic experience, but it looks clear, they understood Tati and Sonjay where responsible.

Mr. Watson asked if there was anyone else in the house. I said Roe was upstairs sleeping. I didn't mention MJ. I knew that would be a whole different can of worms. We sat in pure silence covered in a blanket. We watched as they brought out bodies and evidence. Mr. Watson said he knew something wasn't right with this group and he was glad it has all ended. He was so naive. I was smart enough to know things were far from over.

I still had to deal with the business and Jas. The backyard lights came on and a cute chocolate woman came marching over holding a microphone. A camera man was hanging on her heels. She finally reached us greeted us. "Hello, I am India Lee and I am here to catch the tea on the street. From my understanding this may be a love quarrel gone wrong. Is that correct?" She asked as she extended the microphone towards me. I looked like a deer caught in headlights. I couldn't say anything. I was on live t.v. Jodi must have saw I was losing it.

She jumped right in and took over the interview. Mr. Watson noticed my discomfort and grabbed me by the hand and lead me to the front. He apologized for everything that had taken place and that if he needed anything he would follow up with me. I told him to take his time. I was tired of hearing from him. He laughed and reassured he thinks he had everything he needs at this point and wanted me to get home safely. I hopped in the car and just as he was about to close the door, Jodi joined me.

"Mind if I catch a ride?" She asked. I laughed and told her she could join me. The driver closed the dividing mirror and we began to roll out. We were getting out of there. Once we hit the highway and the blue and red lights were not flashing in the review mirror I stuck my hands in one of my bags and found a joint. I lit it up and took a big pull. I passed it to Jodi. We both sat in silence. I softly began to talk to her.

"Tonight was crazy. This entire week has been overwhelming. Everyone is gone but....Jas." I said realizing I hadn't heard anything from her. Jodi reached over and grabbed my hand. Remember that task I told you I could handle. ... You're welcome." She said. I was surprised. I wanted to ask questions about how it happened but it wasn't the time nor place to discuss it. The remaining ride back to my place was silent. We watched the news on the TV's that where embedded in the ceiling. Turns out even the reporter had a long night. This wasn't her first story of the evening.

I knew she looked familiar. She covered that story I wanted to watch earlier. The dinner date or something like that. Jodi and I spent the remaining ride zoned out. She was still holding my hand. I had to admit her touch was so soothing. I knew I wasn't in harm at the moment but it felt secure. She would even squeeze my hand if we road over a pothole. I guess Jodi proved herself like she said she would. I had no other choice but to let her come back and work with me.

We would have to find her the perfect position. She was all I had left. Literally there was no one standing but me and one of my original enemies. Who would have thought? I know I wouldn't have ever seen this coming. Reality was only the strongest survive.

When its your time, its just your time. Thoughts of letting El Fetched go crossed my mind as we rode past the downtown area. It didn't have the same feeling and meaning behind it all. Reminiscing caused me so much sorrow.

I had accomplished so much and defeated so many obstacles. I am still here. I am still standing. Who said El Fetche had to be an actual building? Maybe It could be just what it is. A fetish. It was time for something new. Nina two point O. We rode off into the sunset without a worry in the world. I was passed out from all the activities of the evening. The ride felt like it was going on forever. When I woke up Jodi was trying to help me get out the truck.

I opened my eyes as much as I could but the sun was too blinding. Once they adjusted and my feet were rooted to the ground, I realized I wasn't home. In fact, I was surrounded by water and beautiful trees. How did we make it to the beach? Jodi held onto my hand. She shut the door and then got down on one knee.

"I have been in love since the day I met you. Let's build something new, fresh. Will you join me?" She asked.

I simply responded. Yes!

www.ingramcontent.com/pod-product-compliance
Lightning Source LLC
Chambersburg PA
CBHW071714140626
46557CB00011B/251